DUDLEY PUBLIC LIBRARIES

The loan of this book may be renewed if not required by other readers, by contacting the library from which it was borrowed.

D1333296

000000596859

DUDLEY PUBLIC LIBRARIES	
000000596859	
Bertrams	26/02/2013
	£18.99
	SED

THE FINAL COUNTDOWN

ALSO BY SHEILA QUIGLEY

Run for Home
Bad Moon Rising
Living on a Prayer
Every Breath You Take
The Road to Hell
Thorn In My Side
Nowhere Man

To find out more visit:

www.theseahills.co.uk

THE FINAL
COUNTDOWN

SHEILA QUIGLEY

www.theseahills.co.uk

First Published in 2012 by Burgess Books
Copyright © Sheila Quigley 2012
All rights reserved
The moral rights of the author have been asserted

This is a work of fiction. Names and characters are the product of the author's imagination and any resemblance to actual persons, living or dead, is entirely coincidental.

No part of this book may be reproduced or transmitted in any form or any means without written permission from the copyright holder, except by a reviewer who may quote brief passages in connection with a review for insertion in a newspaper, magazine, website or broadcast.

British Library Cataloguing in Publication Data:
A catalogue record for this book is available from
the British Library.

ISBN-13: 9780956654663

Printed and bound in the UK by
TJ International Limited, Cornwall, PL28 8RW.

Burgess Books
Houghton-le-Spring
United Kingdom

www.burgessworld.co.uk

DEDICATION

For Gary on Holy Island, who never sold a book in his life, and is now an expert.

ACKNOWLEDGEMENTS

This one's for my readers, wherever you are, near and far.

THE FINAL COUNTDOWN

PROLOGUE

NORFOLK
60 AD

Fresh from the battle of Camulodunum, a woman strode into the crowd at dusk. She paused for a moment and looked around, before mounting the small hill so that she could be seen by all. The setting sun picked out the red strands in her waist-length brown hair as the wind whipped it around her face. She was a tall woman and wore a many coloured shawl around her shoulders, held together at the front with a large brooch. Around her neck there was a golden torc. Her bearing was regal, as suited a queen. Her name was Boudicca.

The Iceni tribe belonged in what is now Norfolk. They had just lost their king, Boudicca's husband. Her daughters had been raped, and Boudicca's body held the marks of the beatings she had endured. The land had reverted to the Romans on the death of the king. And the Iceni were in revolt.

They were now on their way to Londinium, but as she urged her countrymen on, Boudicca had a hidden agenda. She held a secret title, that of Keeper of the Book. A book that had been stolen from her, a book that held the names of an elite set of families. A book that she must take possession of at all costs.

A few hours later Boudicca lay down her sword. From her chariot she looked around. Four men had been sent out to search the four corners of Londinium. The dust of battle was settling but of the men there was no sign.

Anxiously she spun round full circle, then out of the dust they came. One of the men, the third that she checked out, was carrying something. The others were empty handed.

'Could it be?' she muttered, hope rising in her heart as she jumped down from her chariot.

The soldier reached her and handed over the parcel. It was wrapped and bound tightly in a blanket of woven horse-hair. Slowly, with trembling hands, Boudicca unwrapped it.

A moment later she held it against her chest, and smiled as she said, ' Thank God... It is the book.'

The soldiers bowed their heads

'One day, a man born here and yet to be a saint will come home from his journeys. Then he will set off once more and take the book to an Island in the North East of this land, where it will be safe, until it is needed. We are charged with the safe keeping of the book, but,' she looked up from the book, 'first give the order that Londinium is to be razed to the ground.'

Boudicca and her army went on to sack Verulamium. However, the Iceni were to be defeated by Suetonius in the battle of Watling

Street. After fighting bravely for hours, and seeing what was about to happen, Boudicca called her four trusted guards.

'We must go now, the book is too precious to be taken from us again. It must be saved so that our future generations do not live by the yoke.'

Together they left the battlefield.

Boudicca was never seen again.

PART ONE

NORTHUMBERLAND
Present Day

CHAPTER ONE

'OK... That's it, enough. I need rest, the whole world's gone fucking crazy today,' Detective Kristina Clancy said to the blonde police driver, Susan Cleverly. Her own car was in the garage again, and she had to use Susan, whom she had come to like. She found the woman quite friendly, if a trifle nosy at times, but she put it down to wanting to know more about how detecting really worked.

'You can say that again.' Cleverly took her keys out of her pocket and jingled them, hoping that Kristina would get the hint.

'You'll be worn out as well.'

Cleverly nodded, and stifled a yawn.

'Right. Seeing as there's nothing more we can do here, time for home.' Together they turned and headed for the police car.

And it had been a long day for them all, a day in which they had dealt with a gruesome double murder, where the victims, two young men, had been found near the river Tweed in the early hours by a couple on their way home from the local night club.

Kristina suspected that they weren't really a couple as such, seeing as they hardly seemed to even know each other's names, but were wondering down by the river for something much more than an early morning stroll.

They had both been let go after a few hours. Kristina was convinced they had nothing to do with the murders, they had just been the unlucky ones to find them. Basically they had been in the wrong place at the wrong time, and they had both been seriously traumatised by the state of the bodies. She'd also rejected the thought that the murders could have something to do with the Families, a group of people that Mike Yorke was out to prove ruled the world and had done for centuries, keeping the world and its people under a ruling class they did not even know existed.

Kristina pictured the bodies and shuddered. Both of them had been horrifically tortured to death, their faces unrecognisable, and then their tongues had been cut out and placed on their chests - probably while they were still alive, the pathologist had informed her. There was no apparent motive as yet, though Kristina had mulled over the thought that it seemed to be a warning of sorts, and one which the news sources would have a field day with, when-if- they found out.

But Kristina was trying her best to keep a tight lid on everything, telling her superiors that this was exactly what the murderer wanted, the warning out there.

But who he was warning was up for grabs.

She guessed that whoever the murderer was would be chafing at the bit wondering when it was going to be made public, and the longer they kept it quiet, the more chance there would be of the murderer going back to the spot to see if the bodies were still there.

Then, if that hadn't been enough, some utterly stupid boy racer, hyped up on drugs, had decided that speed - in more ways than one - was a great thing, even though the heavens had opened for hours at a time, causing flash flooding on most of the motorways in the north of England.

The idiot had thought that doing way over a hundred on the flooded A1 was the way to get his kicks, sending walls of spray up and over the roof of his car and many others. That was, until he crashed head on into a bus full of very unlucky old people, who had been out for a fateful day trip to the Northumberland coast.

Unable to control the car, he'd crossed the road and hit the bus full on, killing the bus driver and five passengers and injuring most of the others. The catalogue of broken bones was immense. It had taken hours to sort out, and because of staff shortages due to government cuts, Kristina had personally visited all the families of the dead. The colossal fool of a car driver had got off with a few cuts and bruises, and was now cooling his heels in one of the cells. If Kristina had her way, the prick would never get out. Remorse was something the dickhead had never heard of, Kristina had thought, as she'd slammed the cell door behind him.

To finish the day nicely, a domestic in Berwick had threatened to get out of hand, with the woman swearing she would throw herself out of the bedroom window of a fourth-floor flat. Thankfully, after an hour or so, she'd been talked down by the negotiator, a middle aged man by the name of Melvin Kingstone, who Kristina had never met before. Annoyingly, he kept asking her where the hell Mike Yorke was, frustrating Kristina even more.

In the end, things ended amicably enough. Until the next time, Kristina thought, looking at the highly-strung young woman as she got into the car and told Cleverly to head for home.

Most never jump. It's attention that they want, and now that she's had it once, I can guarantee it'll happen again. Shaking her head as they drove past the unneeded ambulance, she gave Stan, one of the drivers, a wave. Smiling at her, he blew her a kiss.

Now, finally arriving home, and just as she was about to put her feet up and watch a bit of telly to take her mind off the missing Mike Yorke, there was a sudden loud knocking on the door.

'Shit,' Kristina moaned, as she used the TV remote to shut Keith Lemon up. 'What the hell now?'

She opened the door to find Mr Brodzinski standing there. Oh no, Kristina thought. I can't be dealing with this now.

Mr Brodzinski, a chess-playing friend of Detective Jason Cox, had a missing grand-daughter who had been held in the monastery near Holy Island with many others, against their will. The teenagers had been plied with drugs to keep them compliant, as well as work-ing them to death in the drug sheds. They had been treated as slaves and used any way he wanted. The culprit, who was now on the run, was known simply as The Leader. Mr Brodzinski's grand-daughter

Annya was now presumed dead.

'How did you...?'

'I followed you home.'

Inwardly Kristina sighed as she said, 'Mr Brodzinski, I'm sorry for your loss, but it's against the law to follow a police officer home. And Sergeant Rafferty is actually in charge of your case.'

She felt lousy being so short with the old man, but there were lines that shouldn't be crossed, and following and visiting a detective at home was definitely one of them. Especially after the fucking day she'd just had!

'Don't like her.' He shuffled his feet for a moment. 'And really, dear, frankly I do not trust the woman. There is something that is not quite right about her.'

Hmm, not keen on her myself, Kristina was thinking. Never liked her from day one. Arrogant isn't the word for her. But she said, 'There really isn't a lot I can do, Mr Brodzinski, as I said befor...'

'My grand-daughter is most definitely not dead, Detective,' Mr Brodzinski interrupted her. 'I feel her.' He patted his chest. 'In here... She is not dead. I know.'

'But--'

He shook his head, as he went on insistently. 'There are no buts, Detective, no buts at all. My Annya is not dead.'

Kristina sighed. 'You have spoken with Detective Cox, haven't you, Mr Brodzinski? I thought you and he were friends.'

'We have spoken, yes, but he is of the same mind as you and says it is up to the other one if the case remains open. Though he did say he would try and talk to her about it, and he has.'

'And what did Sergeant Rafferty say to him?'

'She has closed the case. So now I have come to you.'

'Oh. Well.' Kristina did feel sorry for him, but with resources stretched as tight as they were, and with government cuts starting to bite deep, and Mike Yorke missing, she needed Rafferty on the double murder case.

She hesitated for a moment, trying to think of a way to let him down gently. Unable to come up with anything as the old man was staring intently at her, she said, 'Tell you what, Mr Brodzinski. I'll have a word with Sergeant Rafferty myself, and see if I can get her to take another look at things, perhaps question some of the other kids who were in the monastery at the same time as your grand-daughter. You never know, one of them might come up with something... Perhaps.'

Rafferty can spare an hour or two, surely, Kristina thought, as she smiled at Mr Brodzinski.

'Thank you.' He bowed his head. 'That is all that I ask, that my Annya is not forgotten.' He went to turn away, then, looking back at Kristina, he again touched his chest. 'She is in here. Alive. I know.'

Kristina nodded and watched silently as he walked away, head down and shoulders hunched. She'd seen parents, grandparents and other family members in denial before, but something about this man touched her. Thoughtfully she closed the door and went into the kitchen. A cup of tea, then she would give Rafferty a ring. It wouldn't hurt her to give the case another look over, for God's sake. She glanced at her watch. Would she be home now?

She had no idea if the other woman had any social life at all, or even if she had any hobbies. In fact, she suddenly realised just how little she did know about Sergeant Rafferty. The woman had simply appeared in the office one morning, supposedly on exchange from the Dublin Garda, her superior assuring her that she had been informed of Rafferty's coming over a week beforehand, and that the email must have been lost.

'Hmm,' she muttered, thinking of ways to put that right. First thing in the morning, she would get Cox onto it. Any missing emails, she was sure he'd be able to find them.

But for now a cuppa, then a quick chat with Rafferty. After all, it was part of the main case, which was still very ongoing. Even though they'd been told from above to drop a few things, which she and Cox had both found very puzzling. Plus there was no body. Really, there was nothing to prove that the kid was dead, which made Rafferty way out of order. Annya Brodzinski should be listed as missing.

Why? Why sign a kid off, when there was no proof?

Shaking her head, she reached over the blue Formica bench to switch the kettle on. There was another knock on the door. 'For Christ's sake!' She practically stomped to the door.

Pulling it open, she blinked in surprise to find Detective Cox standing there.

'I've got things to tell you, and no, they won't wait - can't wait.' He pushed his way past her.

This was very un-Cox-like. Kristina, following him into her sitting room, frowned, wondering what the hell was up now. Whatever he'd found out, he was very excited about it.

Not long after, and deep in thought, Kristina slowly closed the door behind Cox. Both were colleagues and very good friends of Detective Inspector Mike Yorke, who had suddenly and under suspicious circumstances disappeared.

She leaned heavily against the door. Feeling the weight of the world on her shoulders and a slightly queasy feeling in the pit of her stomach, her fear for Mike Yorke becoming stronger by the minute, she sighed, knowing that staring into space and dwelling on what might or might not be was definitely not an option. Certainly not in this frightening new world that Mike, and now Cox, had made into a nightmarish reality.

With a final sigh, she pushed herself away from the door and made her way into the sitting room, glancing at the tiny square-faced silver clock on the mantelpiece which, like most other things in the small cosy two bed roomed cottage in the border town of Berwick on Tweed, had belonged to her beloved grandmother, Margaret. Kristina sighed. Her grandmother had died over three months ago leaving everything she had to her and a cousin, named Margaret after her grandmother. Cousin Margaret lived in London and worked on some beauty magazine. She had not been in touch with their grandmother for at least seven years, and hadn't even been bothered to come to the funeral, but she was now demanding Kristina sell the house.

Yeah, well, she can flaming well dream on, cheeky cow. I'm not moving, not again. She sighed. It seemed as if all she had known this year had been trouble and death.

Nine o'clock. She tutted as her eyes focused in on the clock, then, shaking her head again, muttered, 'Where the hell are you, Mike? What is going on? Why the hell didn't you explain more? It's damn hard adding the pieces up.'

Small in stature, with a magnificent mane of auburn hair, Kristina flung herself onto the brown leather settee. She stretched the kinks out of her neck muscles, and pulled her red t-shirt down over her jeans before putting her hands behind her head and staring at the ceiling, mulling over what Cox had just told her.

Detective Cox was a computer whiz, and he'd done some fishing around for Mike. What he'd come up with had been frightening, and unbelievable to say the least. But it fitted in with the little Mike had actually told them. Problem was, he had found out just what Mike had asked him to find but, seeing as Mike was AWOL, there was no way to pass the information on.

'No way,' she muttered, her mind jumping back to what Cox had told her.

'He must have got it wrong. Must have, too many movies and late night snacks. No way can what he dug up be true, even if it does fit in with everything.' Cox was a known grazer of junk food. Kristina and the rest of the team often ribbed him about his diet which Cox, being Cox, he took good-naturedly.

Her gut feeling, though, said the opposite. Cox was also the most unimaginative and down to earth person she'd ever met. To come up with something like this would mean he'd had a serious personality transplant. Sitting up, she sighed and chewed on her thumbnail.

Recently widowed, Kristina had only just came back to Berwick on Tweed. The moment she saw Mike, after a three year absence, she knew that the flame, despite her marriage, was still burning as strong as it ever had.

Stupid that I left in the first place!

And if I'm honest, he's the real reason I came back here.

Even if I truly didn't plan it.

Well, not consciously.

But, where the hell?

She picked up her mobile and tried his number again. After a minute, and no answer, frustrated she threw the phone down on the settee and glared at it as if it was to blame for everything wrong in the world, as well as the missing Mike Yorke.

'Where the hell are you, Mike?' she muttered again. 'Stubbornest man I every flaming well met. You always bloody well were!'

A moment later she sat upright. 'Shit, nearly forgot to phone Rafferty.' She picked up the phone and dialled Rafferty's number. After a few rings, it went to voicemail. 'Hmm.' Kristina looked at the phone and shrugged. 'I'll try again later.'

She sighed. Forgot to tell Cox to look into Rafferty as well, and about the missing email that could or could not be lost. Too tired, she thought, as she massaged her temples.

'Time for bed.'

Only a few minutes had gone by since she'd closed the door on Cox, and as she spoke out loud she heard a quick, sharp bang. With a puzzled frown, and her mind notching up a gear, she went to the window. Her back against the wall, she carefully opened the curtain from the side and peeked out.

She frowned. What the--?

Cox's car was still parked outside the house. The night was damp and slightly foggy, with a mist from the north sea which had closed in earlier in the day, but with the aid of the street lamp outside her door she could just about see him through the misted-up car window.

Hmm, she thought, what's he still hanging about for? There'll be hell to pay when he gets home, and that's a fact. Cox's wife is the one who wears the pants in his house alright.

Suddenly she froze. Was that a sound close to her front door, or was she just imagining it?

No, definitely not, I'm hearing things. She half-convinced herself. But again, a moment later she thought she heard something. The flesh on the back of her neck began to tingle, and a slight flush of fear ran down her spine.

Why hasn't Cox moved?

What the hell is going on?

The sound, which was hard to identify, but which she imagined was a bit like someone furtively trying the door handle without much success, happened again.

OK, the door handle is stiff and quirky, but did I lock the door?

'Shit!' she muttered, thinking back to when she closed the door after Cox and realizing that no, she hadn't locked the door behind him. She quickly looked around for a weapon, something, anything she could use to defend herself with.

If there really is someone creeping about.

If I'm not just imagining it.

There's nobody there.

Of course not.

But why hasn't Cox moved?

Bet he just fell asleep, it's this whole fucking business, got me spooked to high heaven.

And then she heard the sound again.

Her breath caught in her throat.

CHAPTER TWO

Mr Brodzinski walked to the crossing at the end of the road where, after a white van went speeding past, he crossed over and made his way towards a small café. Bright green neon lights in the window advertised the café's name, Marco's. It was a few doors down on the opposite side of the road to Kristina's house.

He ordered coffee and a piece of chocolate cake, then went and sat in one of the window seats. The seats were wooden but had comfortable lemon cushions with white stripes on them, which matched the walls and the lemon and white checked table cloths.

What to do now? He was thinking, as the coffee and chocolate cake were placed in front of him by a young woman with a smile that sadly reminded him of his grand-daughter. He added cream to the coffee and picked up the fork to eat his piece of cake.

'My Annya is not dead,' he muttered, the cake halfway to his mouth, his lips barely moving, unheard by the two young girls sitting at the next table, heads and mobile phones together, doing their own brand of muttering.

He stirred the coffee and took a drink, relishing the taste and loving the smell. He smacked his lips. Ah, this was good coffee. He took another sip and looked out of the window, watching as a car he recognised pulled up outside the detective's house. His hopes lifted as he saw his friend Cox get out of his car.

Detective Clancy must have phoned him.

Perhaps they are going to sort it together.

Cox did promise me he would do what he could.

With a feeling of excitement stirring his blood, he swung his head round to the clock on the wall, then to a notice board next to the clock for the opening times.

Hmm, half an hour left before closing.

He would sit it out, wait as long as he had to until their business was finished, then when they came to the door, go over and confront them. Even if he had to stand outside when the café closed, for however long.

My Annya is not going to be forgotten!

CHAPTER THREE

Kristina's eyes fell on a set of ornamental swords that she'd told her grandmother to hand in to the police station a few years ago, which of course the lovely awkward old bugger never had. Kristina had been meaning to, ever since she'd moved back down here, only she kept forgetting. Quickly she crossed the room and pulled the top sword out of its sheath. She judged it to be not quite a meter long, quite heavy and looked rather sharp. She had a very quick mental picture of her grandmother sharpening the blade.

Just the sort of thing she would do, even though they're illegal, thank God no one had been stupid enough to break in they would have met a worthy opponent in grandma alright. Kristina thought as, light-footed, she ran to the cream leather settee along the wall beside the door. Jumping up, she stood and took a moment to steady herself. One knee bent, one bare foot firmly planted on the arm of the settee and the other on a cushion, she raised the sword above her head with both arms. Making sure she had the balance right, she waited, straining her hearing. It had gone deathly quiet. She could hear nothing.

If there is someone there, they're good!

The door handle slowly began to turn. Kristina puffed the air out of her cheeks then, taking a deep breath, she held it in, pushing her worries for Cox and Mike to the back of her mind as self preservation kicked in and she gripped the handle of the sword even tighter.

The door opened, and the first thing Kristina saw was the gun. Gathering all her strength, without hesitating she brought the sword down in a quick slanted movement. Her aim was not to kill, but to knock the gun out of whoever's hand it was, and to disable the bastard and put herself at the advantage.

The gun flew up into the air, and to Katrina's horror it took her would-be assailant's thumb with it. As the gun spun over and over, droplets of blood spread in a wide arc, splattering the walls and furniture. Then gravity took over, and the gun fell in a direct line to the floor. The thumb landed at the shocked man's feet a second later, tip first, then falling over.

Kristina was just as shocked as the man, whose face had drained of all colour as he clutched his wrist tightly with his left hand, and stared at her in utter disbelief.

Overcoming her shock and moving quickly, Kristina jumped for the gun. She landed on her knees. Her fingers were closing round the handle when the first kick hit her ribs.

'Bitch!' he screamed. 'Fucking bitch!' His face creased with pain, he glared at her through thick dark-rimmed glasses as his whole body began to shake.

Rolling with the kick, Kristina managed to grab the gun, but she wasn't quick enough to avoid the next kick. It landed at the base of her spine, right on her tail bone, sending spasms of pain all the way up her back.

Screaming, but without hesitating, she quickly rolled over and, still on her knees, aimed the gun at his crotch, just as his foot raised and he was about to kick her again.

'Freeze, you bastard!' she yelled, pulling herself up from the floor by gripping the settee arm with her right hand, and managing to hold the gun steady with her left.

'Not much else I can do, is there?' he said with a sarcastic sneer. 'The odds, as they say, are in your favour.' The overwhelming smell of garlic as he spoke turned Kristina's stomach. But she guessed he was babbling to stop himself from screaming. Professional to the end - if a tad sarcastic.

'Take your trousers off, scumbag.'

'What?'

'You heard. Drop them.'

'You're serious, aren't you?' He looked at her as if he still couldn't believe what had just happened.

'Deadly. Now drop them.'

Holding his right hand, which was bleeding heavily, tight against his chest, he loosened the belt buckle on his dark grey trousers with his other hand and, with a sneer, pulled his zip down. His trousers dropped to his ankles.

'OK. Step out of them, then drop the underpants.'

'You for fucking real, or what?' Again he glared at her in disbelief.

'Just do it now. And don't for one minute think I don't know how to use this.'

Outside, Kristina appeared calm and totally in control of the situation, but inside she was terrified. Knowing that no way could she let him see just how frightened she was, she waved the gun at him. 'Move it.'

Grinding his teeth in anger, he slowly rolled his underpants down and stepped out of them.

'OK, get the rest off. Oh - and that's nothing special down there, by the way. Really nothing to be proud of.'

Kristina could have bitten off her tongue when she saw the anger on his face.

Shit! Shouldn't have said that!

But it was her way of dealing with danger. It was how she kept control. And it wasn't every day, even in the police force, when you were faced with a semi-naked, heavily bleeding, thumbless man.

'Kick the trousers over.'

'I'm bleeding to fucking death here, bitch, and you want to play fucking bedroom games?'

'With you? Er, that'll be a big fat no. Kick 'em over, scumbag.'

Kristina had never considered herself as foolhardy, or a hero. Well aware that the incident with the thumb had been a freak accident that could probably never be repeated in a million years, she walked slowly backwards, her eyes locked steadily on the man's, until her hip made contact with the phone table. Finding the phone blindly by scrabbling around with her free hand, she picked it up and quickly dialled 999.

'OK, sit,' she said, after putting her call through.

His jaw dropped, and he blinked repeatedly as he said, 'Aren't you even going to phone a fucking ambulance for me, you stupid fucking ginger cow?'

'Nice! There's an ambulance on the way, prick, you heard me ask for one. Though I doubt you would have phoned one for me if things had turned out the way you expected them to.' She waved the gun again. 'Now fucking do as you're told, and friggin' well sit down now before I lose it altogether.'

The man, who had made no attempt to remove any more of his clothing, sat down quickly, swearing under his breath.

Heart pounding, wondering if she was doing the right thing, Kristina put the gun on the table beside the phone. She hurried over and pulled his belt from his trousers, watching him closely and praying he wouldn't suddenly make a move.

'At least light me a cigarette up, they're just in my top pocket.'

'Do you think I'm stupid?'

He frowned at her as she went on with a slightly shaking hand. 'Hold your hands up.'

The frown turned to a smirk as he sensed that she wasn't quite as in control as she'd have him believe. He raised his hands little more than an inch, and spat at her contemptuously, 'I can take you any time, bitch.'

'Move them now, or else,' Kristina yelled. Trying to convince herself that she was in charge, she was thinking, if you coulda, you woulda, mate!

She noticed that he was using his left hand as a tourniquet for his missing thumb, not that it was doing much good the blood was running fast. Staring at her with more than a touch of hate in his eyes, he raised his hands another six or seven inches. Quickly she wrapped the belt around his wrists, and pulled tight, knowing that she really should have tied his hands behind his back, but fearing he might bleed to death. And this bastard needed to be brought to justice. Gritting her teeth, she pulled the belt even tighter, helping to slow the blood flow to his hands.

As she leaned in closer, he moved his head forward, trying to nut her between her eyes and just missing her nose.

'Bastard,' he snarled.

Kristina jumped out of his reach, and back-pedalling to the table she grabbed the gun.

'Try that again, mister.' She waved the gun at him. Wiping the blood off her own hands with his trousers, she flung them to the far corner of the room, then picked his underpants up and threw them into the opposite corner, figuring that if he did manage to escape, every second taken up would be a bonus.

'I'll look forward to cutting your tongue out, woman,' he said, as

Kristina headed for the door.

Intent on getting away, she grabbed her black coat and her handbag from the coat stand and went quickly through the door, She was shrugging into her coat as she reached the car, and Cox. She shoved the gun quickly into her pocket as fearing the worst, her heart pounding, she opened the car door.

Cox, who had been leaning on the door, slumped to the side and was in danger of falling out. He was either unconscious or dead, she didn't know which, but his face was covered in blood. Slowly, as if in slow motion, his body slipped further out of the car.

'Cox! Cox, wake up. Please wake up.'

Kristina gave a small sob, although the thought that Cox might be dead, killed by the semi-naked man in her house, had crossed her mind. Faced with the truth of what she had feared rocked her to the core. A moment later she froze, when she heard the sound of sirens in the distance.

'What the--' She had been adamant, when she'd phoned in, that under no circumstances at all were there to be any sirens - not even from the ambulance, in case they alerted anyone who was with the gunman, hiding in the area.

Quickly, aware that every second counted, she pulled Cox from the car, and placed him in the recovery position. His mobile phone fell out with him and hit the side of the kerb. Kristina picked it up and shoved it into her pocket, alongside the gun, figuring that he must have been using the mobile when he'd been shot.

If only he hadn't sat outside for those precious minutes to talk to whoever he'd phoned, he might be alive now.

She was muttering over and over, 'Sorry, Cox, sorry.' As gently as she could, she kissed her middle and forefingers and placed the kiss on his cheek. Thanking God that the keys were in the ignition, she jumped in the car and, engine screaming, reversed up the street in the opposite direction to the sirens.

It killed her to leave Cox without knowing if he was alive or dead, even though she strongly suspected the latter, but she had to get away, and quickly. And she had to find Mike.

CHAPTER FOUR

Mr Brodzinski starred in horror as Kristina screeched up the road in Cox's car. He'd watched Cox come out of the house and get in his car, and had been about to cross over the road, cursing himself for not going over sooner - he'd really wanted to catch them both together, and get a solemn promise from both of them. Then just as he'd been about to step off the path, another man had approached the car. He and Cox seemed to be talking for a moment or two, but Brodzinski's eyesight was not what it had once been. He'd seen the man in the thick rimmed glasses point at Cox with a newspaper draped over his hand, then jumped a second later when he'd heard the muffled bang. He'd frowned in puzzlement when the man dropped the paper, but was still holding something in his hand as he ran up the half-dozen steps to the house.

Brodzinski strongly suspected it was a gun, but shied away from the fact. That sort of thing only happens in films, or books! Besides, if he believed what his eyes were telling him, it meant that the man had shot his friend. Cox might even be dead!

Staring over at Cox in the car, Brodzinski didn't know what to do. He was still debating with himself when Kristina had burst out of the house as if all the devils in hell were pursuing her.

And now Cox was lying on the ground across the street. This time he was faced with no choices. For some reason, his friend was lying there, and there was only one thing he could do. He stepped into the road just as the first police car came flying round the corner. Quickly he put his foot back on the path and quietly stepped back into the shadows, trying to ease his conscience with the thought that the professionals would know better what to do than he ever would.

Something strange was going on, though, he knew that much. Another police car, followed by an ambulance, came round the corner, and the scene was lit up with red and blue flashing lights. But it was something he certainly didn't want to get involved in. His first duty was to his grand-daughter. He stepped further back until he was hidden from the road by the hedge.

He really hoped his friend was all right. Cox was a good man, and a good friend but his time was precious. He needed every minute for Annya, and getting mixed up with whatever this business was, would be no help to her.

Unless it was all connected?

He watched silently as Cox, who hadn't moved, was put onto a stretcher, and the ambulance pulled quickly away. He breathed a sigh of relief and tried to shrug the guilty feeling away. Though if Cox was dead, he would feel guilty that he had not done his bit to help, for the rest of his life.

Then the man in the thick glasses, who had been talking to Cox before he went into the policewoman's house, was helped by a policeman, with his hand on his arm, down the steps and into a police car which took off with all lights flashing.

Was that blood all over his clothes?

Puzzled as to what he'd witnessed, and knowing it hadn't made much sense - the man, Brodzinski was sure now, had definitely been bleeding heavily - he hung around for another fifteen minutes, just in case the man with the glasses had a friend come looking for him and pounced on anyone around.

Finally satisfied that no one else was coming, he left his hiding place and headed home.

LONDON

CHAPTER FIVE

Two hours had passed since Smiler had run from the safe house, two gruelling hours in which he had endured pure torment. With the gait of an old man, shoulders hunched, head dropped, and heart aching so bad it was a real physical pain in his chest, he'd stumbled past houses, shops, parks, and ended up in this draught-ridden doorway. He'd tried to piece together everything Rita had told him. And he still couldn't get his head around most of it.

Jesus! It was stupid to think that anyone could get away with that sort of thing now.

Perhaps thirty centuries ago!

But now?

Impossible!

'Impossible, to think that the whole fucking world was…Is, living a lie,' he muttered, shaking his head slowly and watching a large spider scuttle away when he moved his foot.

Rita had told him so much he still couldn't get his head round most of it. He knew that he felt angry, very angry, and that made him understand the total need for secrecy. Anger is deadly. If everyone suddenly found out, then the world as we all know it would no longer exist. The transition had to be smooth, and certain people had been working towards this for years.

Having taken refuge from the relentless drizzle which had started not long after he'd run, he now sat huddled in the shop doorway, his knees up to his chest and his head tucked in, his arms wrapped around his legs as he rocked from side to side, a harsh sob escaping every few minutes from his burning lungs.

When he'd heard the full horrendous truth from Rita, he'd been unable to take it. He'd taken flight, pushing everyone and everything out of his way. He'd run as fast as he could away from them all, and ended up here. Just where 'here' was, though, he had no idea.

He'd passed a few other dingy shops before he practically collapsed in this doorway. He knew it was a rough place by the smell of piss, the fag ends and litter lying about, and the paint peeling off the dirty red paint-work he could see peeping out from behind the metal shutters on the door and window, which were covered in graffiti. There were countless spiders scurrying around, and the odd adventurous beetle. He guessed that it was close to one o'clock in the morning, but where the hell was he?

He lifted his head when he heard shouting coming from what he thought was a flat above the shop, and sighed. He'd heard plenty of shouting in his life, a harsh raised voice was nothing new, and he doubted strongly if anyone could come up with something he'd never heard before.

His mother used to shout at him all the time - well, when she was actually conscious, and not in negotiations with some creep or another, haggling over the price of her, or his body. For years he had hated her for the life she'd given him. Not once had he seen the inside of a school. His reading skills had been taught to him by her, and that was only because she used books to escape her own dreary existence. But now he finally knew the reason why she'd been the way she had.

He tried as hard as he could to find some pity for her, but the wounds were still too raw. He shuddered. No one should ever be allowed the life he'd lived.

He'd spent most of that life hating everything and everybody, mostly for no reason, just the fact that they, and he, existed. And then for a short time he'd thought his life was changing. Meeting Mike Yorke had opened his eyes to a different life altogether, to real people, to kindness, to unselfishness, and then to Aunt May.

Living on Holy Island with Aunt May had been a dream come true. At last he'd felt as if life was worth living. He was finally free. Free from the absolute horror of just existing, of being a complete nobody that nobody cared about, just another waif and stray on the streets.

But that bubble had soon burst. Shame on me for thinking it could go on forever. And now Mike Yorke was missing, and a whole new can of worms had opened up. Light filtered down from the flat upstairs, making it quite easy to see. He flicked a tear off his cheek, and rubbed the wetness between his finger and thumb. Then he took his cigarettes out and fumbled in his pocket for his lighter, slightly worried for a moment in case he'd lost it. Then his fingers closed around it, and, pulling the lighter out, he lit up.

He took a huge drag and filled his lungs, holding it for a moment before realising it into the dark sky. A few seconds later, he gasped and his body jumped in shock as the upstairs window exploded outwards, showering glass all around. In the middle of the shower, just a foot from where he was sitting, lay the shattered remains of a heavy crystal flower vase, some of the pieces still trembling. The yellow roses that the vase had held were crushed and scattered. For a moment, he was hypnotised by a large piece of the broken glass as it caught the light. His hand reached out, as his tongue quickly ran across his dry lips.

There was a certain release in the glass, release in the blood that would flow from his body with the aid of that single shiny piece of glass, taking the pain inside away. All he had to do was pick it up. That's all. Just reach out.

Now...Do it!

Easy!

He sighed. His need was huge.

His longing was huge.

Aching inside with the need, and hearing the glass call to him, he stretched out his arm.

His fingers touched the glass. Gently, with his other hand, he brushed a spider away then, with the same finger and thumb that had rubbed the tear off his cheek, he caressed the piece of glass, a small smile on his face.

So easy!

His fingers closed around the glass, and he brought it close to his smiling face. 'So, so easy.

'End it all now, the way out!'

NORWICH

CHAPTER SIX

At the same time as Smiler was contemplating ending it all, a girl he had never met, but who was just as much a victim of the families as he was, woke up.

Shelly Monroe lay on her bed staring at the ceiling. There was a gap in the curtain and the full moon spilled into the room. Tears ran down her face and she didn't have the energy or the strength to wipe them away. Not for the first time, she'd been crying in her sleep.

Everything is such a mess, and it's mostly my own fault, she thought, thinking back to over a year ago when she'd first been introduced to drugs via her friend Alicia and the Leader.

It wasn't fair that everyone thought that Alicia had been a sweet angel. The truth is she had been far from it.

And now I, and Danny, are both in serious trouble.

In fact, we might as well be dead.

As dead as Alicia.

Her heart sank even further. 'Poor Alicia,' she sobbed. 'She didn't deserve what the bastards did to her. At the end of the day, she was a really great girl once, until those pricks got their hands on her. Then, like every other girl or boy trapped by their need, she would do any-thing to satisfy that need.'

She sighed and sat up. She thought she'd been low before, but she had never in her whole life been in such a dark place as this. She felt as if there was nothing left to live for, no reason why, and it was impossible to die.

She'd tried refusing her insulin, but they had only sat on her and injected her themselves, before force-feeding her. Throwing up had-n't helped, because then they had poured sugary drinks down her throat. Everything had been removed from the room. Nothing sharp had been left lying about, even the laces from her shoes had been taken out.

I'm as much a fucking prisoner as I was before!

'Damn.'

If these stupid idiots think they can outwit the families, they're in for a hell of a shock. Because they'll find me, I know they will. It's just a matter of time, that's all.

Tomorrow.

The next day.

They seem nice enough people, but their delusion makes me want to puke and fucking laugh my head off at the same time.

They've been around for centuries, nearly as long as the families have, fighting them in different ways. Oh yes, I just bet they have. Probably as entertainment for the fucking families. Bet the horrible sods piss themselves laughing all the time.

She gripped the sheet angrily, before suddenly gasping. 'That's the way,' she muttered, swinging her legs off the bed.

Why wait for them bastards to come and torture me to death, 'cos whatever the idiots think, I'm not safe here - and neither are they, once the fucking families find them. And they will. This way I'll at least rob them of that satisfaction.

What sort of life have I got now?

Not one worth living, that's a fact.

For a moment she froze as a picture of Danny entered her mind, then jumped to the four of them picnicking down by the river on a hot summer's day, shortly before Alicia introduced her to drugs, and then the Leader.

At the image of the Leader, she shuddered, breaking the spell. She grabbed the sheet and examined it. Finding a tiny hole in one of the corners, she pushed her thumb through and made it bigger, then pulled hard, managing to rip the sheet down to the bottom. Ten minutes later, after much tugging and heaving, she had three strips long enough for what she wanted and quickly began to plait them.

Now, how the hell? She looked up at the ceiling. The house was quite old, built in the last century, and in all the rooms the ceilings were very high. 'Will the light fitting take my weight?' she wondered, staring up at the brass fitting. 'Won't know until I try.'

She grabbed hold of the bedside cabinet and, taking care to be very quiet, she pulled it underneath the light. Climbing on top, she unscrewed the lampshade. After placing it on the floor, she looped the rope sheet twice around the fitting, then around her neck and back over the fitting. For a brief moment, she paused. There were too many thoughts rushing through her head for her to make any sense out of them.

'Just do it,' she muttered.

With sudden determination, she raised one foot, and with the other kicked the cabinet over.

CHAPTER SEVEN

Outside Shelly's bedroom door, Coral sat reading. She loved a good horror story and had a bookshelf full of them, all in alphabetical order. Some of her friends laughed, asking if she hadn't had enough horror in her life. Her stock reply was, 'That's why I read these books, to get a damn good laugh! Most people in this life don't know the true horror of living.'

She paused at a particularly gruesome bit, and turned her head towards the bedroom door.

Is that Shelly moving about? She thought with a frown. Then she heard a loud crash. Quickly, she threw the book down and was on her feet, hurrying into the bedroom.

'Oh, my God,' she gasped, a moment later.

Shelly was hanging in front of her, her legs thrashing back and forth and her eyes bulging out of her purple face. She grabbed Shelly's legs, taking her weight, screaming for Ella to help.

Ella, though, was a heavy sleeper and it took a few minutes for Coral's voice to penetrate. Annya, however, was already awake, the peacefulness of sleep having evaded her yet again. Stumbling out of her bedroom and wondering what all the screaming was about, she yelled down the stairs, 'What's up, Coral?'

'Quick, wake Ella, and bring something sharp.'

'I'm up, Coral.' Ella came out of her bedroom and, hearing Coral's last words, she ushered Annya back to bed.

Oh God, that can only mean one thing, Ella thought, as she ran downstairs and into the kitchen. She pulled the drawer open, only it stuck, too much cutlery in as usual.

'Come on!' she yelled, shaking the drawer in desperation.

Whatever had been blocking it finally moved and the drawer burst open, spilling its contents on the floor. On her hands and knees, Ella frantically tried to find the scissors. Finally spotting them under a couple of white spatulas, she was about to grab them when Annya, who had ignored her about going back to bed, quickly grabbed them, and passing them to Ella they both ran to Shelly's bedroom.

'Shit!' Ella yelled when she entered. Even though it was basically what she expected, it was still a shock. Annya took one look through the door, saw Shelly hanging from the ceiling and, not taking in the fact that Coral was taking most of Shelly's weight, slid down the door in a faint.

Climbing onto the bed and stretching over, Ella quickly cut the rope sheet. Both Shelly and Coral collapsed onto the floor. Above them the light fitting swung from side to side.

Ella untied the rope sheet from Shelly's neck, and checked for signs of breathing. Finding none, she quickly started mouth to mouth.

It took a minute or two, but suddenly Shelly gasped and drew air into her lungs.

'Thank God,' Coral said.

Ella rocked back on her heels. 'What the hell happened?' She looked at Coral. 'Thought we had everything covered.'

Staring at Shelly, Coral shook her head as she puffed the air out of her cheeks. A bashful Shelly rose to a sitting position and put her head in her hands.

'Do we need to send for an ambulance?' Ella asked, staring at Shelly with a worried frown on her face. 'Will she be all right?'

'No, it's fine. She just passed out for a minute.'

'Sure?'

'I am here, you know,' Shelly snapped, lifting her head and staring at Coral.

'And don't we know it,' Coral snapped back, ignoring the frown Ella now threw her way.

'Look, Shelly love.' Coral sighed, then went on more gently, as she rubbed Shelly's shoulder. 'Just about everyone in this house, and those who have passed through it, have been exactly where you are today. That's why we're here to help in every way we can. Trust me, we do know what you're going through. And you aren't the only one who has gone this far, and lived to tell the tale. All over the world people are coming to terms with what happened to them, and they're learning to fight back.'

Ella patted Shelly's hand. 'Talk to us love. Come on, just talk to us. We're here for you,' she said compassionately. 'We'll do everything we can, all of us. You aren't alone any more.'

Somehow this made Shelly feel worse. She stared at Ella's hand and burst into tears.

Coming in from the doorway, Annya paused staring at the distraught girl, she wondered for a monent, what would grandfather do. Crossiong the room she did exactly what she knew he would do. She knelt down and, taking Shelly in her arms, cradled her until her sobs subsided.

CHAPTER EIGHT

Suddenly, as if he'd been stung, Smiler's hand flew to his chest.

'No,' he muttered. 'No…I promised. I promised I wouldn't ever do it again.' His hand shook as if it had a life of its own, or as if a drunken puppeteer had control of it. He slapped his other hand over the top of his treacherous fingers. 'No. I won't do it.' He pictured Aunt May smiling at him, and gathered strength from her image. 'No.'

'Get out!' A man's voice yelled into the quiet, completely breaking the spell the glass had cast over him.

Startled, Smiler dropped the piece of glass as the voice went on, 'I never ever want to see you again. I can't take it any more, You're a fucking crackerjack. Get out.'

'Fuck off.'

'No! I should have listened to my sister. She was right about you all along. Just get out.'

'No, you get out before you follow the fucking flower vase,' a woman screamed in retaliation.

Raising his eyebrows for a moment, Smiler thought, truth be told, I really shouldn't be surprised to find out that the woman is the aggressor. Seen it on more than one occasion.

'Gotta get outta here,' he muttered. 'Not safe!'

He shrugged and gave a small joyless laugh. 'Is anywhere safe?'

Standing up, he waited a moment before creeping silently away from the doorway, his back against the shuttered window, all the while looking cautiously upwards in case the woman followed through with her threat. A few moments later he was at the bottom of the street. Turning, he looked back. Nothing else had followed the flower vase out the window, no bodies lying on the hard ground, and the participants had fallen silent.

'Crazy bastards,' he muttered. Turning back, he took a deep breath and, head down, plodded on.

I wonder if it's me? he was thinking, as he turned into a main street which, after a moment or two staring at the buildings, he recognised.

Hmm. His thoughts drifted back to four or five summers ago. He shuddered. This was where he'd first met a guy named Snakes, just about the evillest person on the whole fucking planet - well, that's apart from the bastards who own the whole fucking place - and this was Snakes' patch.

Not one person, not even his own fucking mother liked Snakes. Smiler remembered the look of fear on her face one day when he'd knocked about with him, and they'd turned up unexpectedly at her house. Snakes had emptied her purse, as well as her pockets, and had even taken the meat pie off her plate, then tipped it up and let the peas and gravy flow onto the table. Not one single word had been exchanged between them. His mother had just stared into space, terrified, her whole body shaking,

For a moment Smiler felt a chill of fear. He took a deep breath. His last parting with Snakes had not been a good one. He remembered the pills trickling into the gutter when he'd thrown them right back in his face.

Shaking the fear off, he diverted his thoughts back to what he'd been thinking before. Anything, anything at all to get the frightening vision of Snakes out of his mind.

It's got to be me, everything I touch.

Everyone I fucking well know, something happens to them.

It's like someone cursed me. He stopped walking and, frustration tearing him apart, he thrust his hands into his pockets.

'Because, actually, truly, I was fucking cursed,' he muttered, remembering what Rita had said about the experiments.

He shook his head, then stared ahead of him at the pubs, even at this dark hour still with their lights blazing out into the night, music blasting loudly and people hovering around the doors. Smokers mostly, he guessed.

He could hear laughing, shouting, the odd snatch of a song, and wondered if he should go on, or turn and head back the way he'd come. After a moment he decided to risk it. The street was full of revellers, with more spilling out of the pubs by the minute, though that meant nothing. There wasn't always safety in numbers, and only fools thought otherwise.

Anyhow, Snakes could be miles away.

Probably on the other side of London, peddling his wares.

Spreading out, picking up more and more stupid silly kids who thought they were invincible, and that they could never become addicted to whatever shit was out there.

Fools!

Once they get a taste of this new shit, it's the beginning of the end.

Sadly, he shook his head and moved on.

Did I listen? he asked himself as, trying to remain invisible, he kept his head down so as not to meet anyone's eyes.

Did I hell!

A few minutes later, he was in the main street. People were criss-crossing from anyone of the five pubs to another. He watched out the corner of his eye as a loud argument between two young semi-naked girls, both obviously very drunk, broke out into a full scale fight. A bouncer, wearing regulation black, yelled across the road to another, standing outside the pub opposite, to help him. The other man was dressed the same, and looked enough like him to be his twin. The fight was quickly quelled when they stepped between the girls, trying to untangle the blonde's fingers from the redhead's mane without getting bitten or scratched by either of them in the process.

Moving quickly past them, Smiler was suddenly stopped in his tracks. Thinking he'd bumped into someone, he hastily stepped back and mumbled an apology.

It was met with an evil laugh, and the feel of cold steel against his neck.

NORWICH

CHAPTER NINE

When Shelly seemed all cried out, Coral helped Annya up and sent her to bed. This time, and still looking very close to tears herself, she complied. Coral helped Shelly into the kitchen while Ella opened a bottle of whiskey. She poured three shots out, then handed them round. 'Better than tea for the nerves.' She raised her glass to Shelly, then quickly downed her drink.

Shelly blinked as, smiling, Coral shook her head.

'OK, so I'm drinking on my own?' Ella asked.

Shelly reached for her glass. Not a lover of spirits, much preferring wine, she did however raise the glass to her lips and knock the drink back as quickly as Ella had.

Shuddering, she looked at Coral, and mouthed, 'Sorry.'

'It's OK kid. You did give us a shock, and I'll probably be walking bent over for the rest of my life.' She rubbed her back and cracked a smile. Shelly twitched her lips in response, but only slightly. In a moment it was gone as if it had never existed, her eyes glazing over as once more she stared into the past.

Ella reached for Coral's glass. 'Right, if you're not drinking, I'll have it. Then I'm off to bed for an hour. Remember, I'm going back in to hell to find out what happens at the family gathering.' The last word she almost spat out, before saying, 'Those laxatives worked a treat on Jasmine. I'm doing a double shift in hell in order to cover for her. Poor bugger. She'll be all right tomorrow, totally unaware of the service she has done mankind.'

She swallowed the whiskey then, giving them both a wave, she said, 'Night, all…what's left of it.'

'Yeah, goodnight, Ella love. Sweet dreams,' Coral replied, while Shelly continued to stare at a space on the wall.

'Oh, they will be short and sweet an' all. Might have time for one or two,' Ella flung over her shoulder.

When she closed the door behind her, Coral turned back to Shelly. 'OK,' she said, then paused a moment when Shelly did not respond. A little louder, she said, 'Shelly.'

Slowly Shelly lifted her head.

'Like I already said, love, you're with friends here. And again, we have all been through what you're going through, but you're not alone, Shelly. You have us.'

Shelly swallowed hard. 'I know. I'm sorry. It's just as they say, it seemed like a good idea at the time.'

'Feeling any better now?'

'Not really.' She intertwined her fingers and pressed them against her chest. 'I…I can't really say how I feel, actually.' She looked up and into Coral's eyes, and paused for a moment before going on. 'Yes,

I can. Dead. That's how I feel, dead. Used and abused…dead!'

Coral nodded sadly. 'Look, it will pass. One day, hopefully soon, you'll wake up and want to fight back. Or…'

'Or what?' Shelly said, before Coral could go on.

Coral took a deep breath, then held her gaze steady with Shelly's for a moment. Sometimes, some of the girls, or the boys, couldn't take the truth that for some of them there was no way back. But Coral was betting on Shelly being strong enough to get there.

'Or,' Coral chewed on her bottom lip, 'sometimes, Shelly, others have succeeded in killing themselves. Sadly, it doesn't matter what we do. The damage is so bad that they can't come back. Sometimes it's because they just aren't strong enough to live with what they've been through.'

'I know how they feel,' Shelly muttered.

'Yes, I know you do.' Coral took hold of both of Shelly's hands. 'But I truly and honestly suspect that you are one of the strong ones… We need you. Shelly.'

Shelly gave her a puzzled look. 'Why?'

'We need you to be a soldier for us, Shelly. We need you to be brave and help us. I think you can do it, Shelly. I think you're definitely one of the strong ones. '

Shelly gave a bitter laugh. 'A soldier? Where do you think we are, in fucking Sunday school? Might as well say you want me for a sunbeam. For fuck's sake.'

'I know you think you know it all, but trust me, you certainly don't. Our network is growing by the day.'

Shelly stood up. 'For fuck's sake, stop kidding yourself, will you? You don't stand a chance.'

Coral smiled. 'Oh yes, we do.'

CHAPTER TEN

Kirill Tarasov surveyed the room as he stepped through the doorway, his eyes angry slits as he looked around the elite of the world for friend or foe. Whichever he saw first would just have to say the wrong word and they would feel the full extent of his anger.

Everyone in the room was wearing evening dress. There was certainly no need of robes or the trappings of secret societies, no need of pagan sacrifices. They were who they were. The families, who had been secretly ruling the world for centuries, the hidden ones who walked amongst the people of the world as bankers, politicians, royalty, lawyers. Judges. These were the ones who made all the decisions, all the rules.

Decisions and rules which benefited only themselves. And they were ruled by greed alone.

He had just stepped out of a helicopter after a mad dash from London, where he'd rescued his oldest illegal son from the grasp of his jealous pathetic excuse for a legal son. The illegal, Mike Yorke, was now on his way, via stretcher, with two family doctors and three guards, to a room at the top of the hotel.

Spotting the shiny baldhead of the American, Slone, Tarasov was making his way towards him when suddenly the horn sounded. He clenched his fists. It would have to wait. Like everyone in the room, he stopped and faced the stage. Luxurious red velvet curtains opened. One golden chair was in the centre of the stage, and the historian, a very tall, thin man with wavy brown hair and eyes far too dark for his pale skin colour, was seated facing them.

As was tradition, the historian asked them all to be seated. He gave them a few minutes, and Tarasov found himself sitting between Prince Carl on his right and the Earl James Henry Simmonds on his left. Prince Carl he could take in small doses if he had to, but the Englishman, Simmonds, he hated.

Simmonds kept his eyes to the front, refusing to acknowledge him, as Prince Carl muttered a quiet, 'Good evening.'

Tarasov nodded in response, crossing his right leg over his left and folding his arms in front of him.

As of tonight, he trusted very few of them. Any one of the twenty-odd family members could have known what his legal son had been up to, anyone of them could have helped him. And anyone of them could be laughing behind his back. Well, let them laugh. They had no idea who he really was, nor what was coming.

He spotted his daughter Lovilla seated in the front row between Count Rene and Slone. As if sensing her father's eyes on her, Lovilla turned around and smiled at him.

What the bloody hell is she doing with them? Tarasov thought, acknowledging her smile with a short nod of his head. His frown deepened and he turned to look at Simmonds.

Simmonds must have seen the movement out the corner of his eye but he choose to ignore Tarasov, and whatever Tarasov was about to say to him was stopped by the historian declaring the extraordinary meeting open.

Five minutes into his speech was as far as he got before he was told to shut up by the American, Slone, who rose and turned to the other family members. 'OK, you all heard him. It has to be done. Don't even know why we had this meeting, anyhow. It was all worked out a long time ago, and things have been in place for centuries.'

Tarasov was immediately on his feet. 'No!' he yelled. 'It's far too barbaric, a plan thought out over a thousand years ago when the world was a different place.'

'A plan already in place.' His daughter Lovilla jumped up and glared at him.

For a brief, barely noticeable moment, Tarasov stalled. Why am I surprised? he thought, before calmly saying, 'Yes - and look at all the death and destruction around the world already.' He ground his teeth together as Slone, who had turned his back to him, an insult in itself, shrugged his shoulders.

'You knew it was happening. You've gone along with it for a long time, so why didn't you say something before now? Suddenly developed a conscience, have you?' Simmonds asked. His lips twisted in a sarcastic scowl.

Tarasov glared at him. 'Perhaps.'

'Perhaps! With your appetites?' He laughed.

'Enough.' Tarasov's voice was loud in the hall.

But Simmonds refused to be silenced. He went on, 'Instead you choose to disturb all of our peace and harass us all, with this fucking stupid unwanted total waste of time meeting.'

The historian chewed on his lip. He'd actually been dreading this meeting. His own family had been linked with the families for generations, the role of historian passed down from father to son.

The very first historian had been a self-taught shepherd with no links to any aristocracy. He was a slave, nothing more, who through time had gained a small trifle of respect, which was passed on to his descendants. Although, throughout history, they could all have been wiped out at any time - the wrong word at the wrong moment, a whisper in an ear, was all it would have taken. Each historian had taken heed of what his father had told him. They were, although not one of them, at least a part of them and the job had always paid very well indeed. And sometimes, just sometimes, when it suited them, they took notice of what he had to say.

Tonight, however, he knew was not going to be one of those nights. Tonight he would sit back and let them get on with it. He refused to take sides, knowing that he and his extended family would more than probably survive what was soon to come. Getting into an argument, taking sides and angering anyone of them, would jeopardize their very existence. If the peasants needed a champion, it was not going to be him.

He sat back and let them argue amongst themselves. When enough time had gone by, he rose. It took a few minutes, because quite a few of the arguments were becoming heated. A lot of them were standing up to emphasize their feelings, with more than one fist raised in anger, but finally silence fell.

He waited until they were all seated again, then he spoke. 'It was written that the start of it all would be in 2011. There would be disaster after disaster, carrying through to 2012.'

'A fucking fairy story.' Someone yelled from the back of the room.

Before the historian could answer, Tarasov was back on his feet. 'It was not written that most of the disasters would actually be started by us, nor the wars deliberately started to cut the population down, long before then. And the greed for oil.'

His last words were met with a few sniggers.

The historian frowned at him. In the sudden silence, a few heads nodded in agreement. One of them was Prince Carl, who rose to stand by Tarasov.

'Yes. it was… More or less,' Slone said.

'Well, seeing as the fools sent to find the true Lindisfarne Gospels still haven't found them, we'll never know, will we?' Prince Carl said.

'We'll find them!' Slone shouted.

The historian sighed and sat back down. It was going to be a very long night.

In the end as he'd suspected, Tarasov and his friends were out-voted. The extermination camps were to be set up at the end of the week.

The cull was about to begin.

No one saw Ella behind the red velvet curtain, hidden in its deep folds. She waited until the historian left his seat, and then hurried to the kitchen, to wander amongst them five minutes later, an innocent slave bearing snacks on a golden tray.

LONDON

CHAPTER ELEVEN

The blade glinted in the streetlight, as it pressed hard against Smiler's throat, so hard he was frightened to swallow. He froze in fear, his eyes wide and staring.

So this is it.

How it's all gonna end.

For a moment sadness overcame his fear, then Snakes spoke.

'Got you now, you fucking little prick,' Snakes sneered at him, his eyes glinting with an evil pleasure.

Smiler gulped, feeling his skin tighten against the pressure. His fear stark in his bulging eyes, he knew that Snakes was capable of anything thinkable, and a whole lot more. And if he was going to kill him, it would be piece by painful piece.

'You owe me big time, and now you're gonna pay. That's the fucking way of it, man.' He laughed, the high-pitched giggle of a madman that would strike fear into the bravest of hearts.

When Smiler heard the hate in Snakes' voice, his legs began to shake, and he felt as if his heart was in his throat, stuck right there alongside the knife.

'No,' he muttered, terrified for his life. 'Please, no. I'll do anything you want.'

Snakes laughed again. 'Huh, begging now, are we, you little bastard? It wasn't that before, though, was it?' He pressed the knife harder against Smiler's throat. 'No one takes the piss outta me, you ugly little twat...Pay time.'

Why did I come this way? Smiler was thinking. Why?

It's my own fucking fault.

Stupid! Stupid! Stupid!

'Move into the alleyway now, fuckface, or else... Move it, if you know what's good for you.'

Snakes applied even more pressure on the knife.

Smiler never felt the knife slice his skin, until he felt a trickle of wetness run down his neck. It was the urge he needed to get moving. Now wondering, as the knife was transferred to his back, if he was ever going to get out of the alleyway alive, he turned and headed in that direction, passing people who never saw what was happening, or people who were pretending not to see what was happening.

When they had gone a few yards into the alleyway, Snakes said, 'OK, freak, stop. Guess this is a good a place as any to do it. Sorry an' all that, but you know how it is on the street. Gotta keep my rep up.' Smiler didn't have to see the smile on Snakes' face, he could hear it in his voice.

For a brief moment he froze as, suddenly, he perversely welcomed the thrust of the blade.

A way out of this terrible existence.

Because that's all I've ever done, is exist.

Really, I was just a fucking experiment!

Do it, he thought. Do it now.

Succeed where I've failed.

He was about to turn and beg Snakes to finish it for him.

The creep will be doing me a favour.

A way out.

Thank you!

But then, from nowhere, came something he hadn't known he possessed until half an hour ago. The face of Aunt May, and a love of the life he'd experienced with both her and Mike Yorke, welled up in him again. That's all he'd ever wanted, in his whole life, he knew that now, someone to care about him. And even though it had only been for a short time, he had found that care in Aunt May and Mike Yorke. And Tiny, he'd never dreamed that you could love a dog so much. Animals had been something to throw stones at, and laugh when they limped off. But that was before, when he was someone else, not as bad as Snakes, but that was the way he'd been heading. Before Mike Yorke and Aunt May. Now he suddenly realised just how much he cared about them all.

Too much to die, just because this bastard wants me to!

His resolve strengthening, and without thinking the consequences through, he suddenly shot his foot forward then back, kicking Snakes hard on his shin, before quickly spinning on his heel to face him. Snakes, shocked that Smiler had summoned up the nerve to defy him, was even more shocked a moment later to see what was rushing down the alleyway towards him.

Staring into Snakes' eyes, and seeing fear, Smiler frowned. He was about to turn to see what was freaking him out, but there was no need. Behind him, he heard a dog growling.

Could it be?

A moment later, he knew by the look on Snakes' face that it was Tiny. Only the sight of the huge dog could terrify him.

His heart leapt. 'Tiny,' he muttered.

Before Snakes had time to get his brain and his feet in motion, Tiny, a Newfoundland/German Shepherd cross, launched himself. In moments, Snakes was on the ground with Tiny's huge paws on his chest and his jaws at his throat.

'Get the fucking monster off me!' Snakes yelled in fear. 'Get him off now! Now!'

'Hold him, Tiny, ' shouted a voice Smiler recognised.

Smiler looked up to see Rita at the top of the alleyway. A huge lump welled up in his throat. Rita too cared about him, else she wouldn't have come looking.

'No,' Smiler said, turning back quickly to face Snakes and the dog. Knowing that Snakes was quite capable of using the law to help himself, by playing the good guy and lying, saying that Tiny had savaged him, and all it would take for Tiny to be put to sleep, his life finished, would be a stupid fool of a judge out of contact with the real world. Smiler yelled, 'He's not worth it, Tiny. Heel. Now, Tiny, come here. Come on, boy, come on.'

Reluctantly, hackles raised and still growling, the dog backed off. But not far, and not once taking his eyes off Snakes, who scrambled to his feet just as Rita got there.

'You all right?' Rita asked Smiler, out of breath as she reached them, and wincing in pain from the pressure that the run had put on her feet and legs. Rita was in love with shoes, especially red ones, and wore the highest heels she could find.

'I am now,' Smiler nodded. Patting Tiny's huge head, he wiped the tears from his eyes with his sleeve. But this time, they were tears of joy. He had never experienced anything like it before.

People actually care about me.

Wow!

As Smiler dealt with these amazing thoughts, and a buzz bigger than anything he'd ever experienced, Rita turned to Snakes. 'On your bike, creep.'

'Fuck off. You're the fucking creep. Look at you,' he sniggered, 'hysterical, how fucking dare you. And that,' he pointed at Tiny, 'I'm having that fucking monster. First chance I get.'

'No, you won't.' Bravely Smiler moved forward. 'No, you won't, 'cos if you touch one fucking hair on his head, I'll have you.'

Backing Smiler up with a stubborn set to her face, Rita stepped closer, and Tiny, as if understanding Snakes' threat, growled deep in his throat. Rita's fists were clenched tightly, and Smiler had never seen her look so angry. She moved forward again until she was face to face with Snakes, who stared defiantly into her eyes. A moment later his face changed as Rita grabbed a fistful of his hoodie top, yanking him even closer.

Nose to nose, she said, 'If I ever see you anywhere near Smiler or the dog again, trust me, you'll regret it. Now move.'

'He owes me.' Snakes spat on the ground.

'He owes you nothing, you lousy scumbag. And I'm not gonna tell you again.' Roughly she thrust him away from her.

Only just managing to stay on his feet, and with a sneer, Snakes turned and shuffled up the alleyway. When he figured he was far enough away to make a run for it if necessary, he turned back. With his forefinger and middle finger he pointed at his eyes and then at Smiler. 'This ain't over, kid.'

Silently Smiler, Rita and the dog stared him down. 'Bastards,' he yelled, before heading around the corner back into the street. 'Fucking bastards.' His voice echoed behind him.

'How…how did you find me?' Smiler asked, still staring at the spot where they had last seen Snakes.

Rita put her hand on Smiler's shoulder, ignoring his flinch. Pointing to her head, she said, 'In here, Smiler. Because you'll always be in here, where ever you are.'

'Thanks,' Smiler said, his head down, hiding a smile.

Rita lifted her hand and put her arm around Smiler's shoulder. 'Come on, Smiler, let's get you back home.'

Nodding and swallowing hard against the lump growing in his throat, Smiler muttered, 'Thank you.'

With Rita's arm across Smiler's shoulders, and Tiny bringing up the rear, they headed for the safe house.

NORTHUMBERLAND

CHAPTER TWELVE

Grim-faced, Kristina made her way to Holy Island, praying that the tide would be out, her thoughts a hopeless jumble of everything Cox had told her. She felt a brief sense of loss. She hadn't known Cox for long, but had come to like him. And Mike always spoke highly of the man, and his wife Samantha, who was so definitely the boss. She had even asked, as if sensing that the chemistry was still there between them both, if she and Mike would come for dinner one night. And that had pleased Kristina no end.

It was hard to think of him dead. Knowing that she hadn't checked properly for life. I should have done more, but surely no one could survive that amount of blood loss.

'It's not really as if Cox is…was…is', she corrected herself quickly, 'known for his fitness regime.'

Why? That was the craziness of it all.

Why kill him?

Though he might not be dead, she told herself again. You don't really know either way, kiddo, he could be alive.

And the reason is because he knew too much!

And now I know too much.

But not enough!

'Oh, my God,' she gasped, suddenly realising just what the man with the gun had said as she'd run out of the house. 'The bastard! He threatened to cut my tongue out!'

Everything fell into place now. The two murdered young people must have known something they had to have. Perhaps they were both in the monastery, either as guards or slaves... Shit!

She gasped. 'He's part of a clean-up crew.'

And that's the reason why that bastard came after me, she told herself, glancing quickly into the rear view mirror.

All clear.

Thank God.

He was going to kill me!

She was heading for Holy Island for two reasons. One was that, a good while back, one night when they had been alone and waiting for Mike to come home from work, Aunt May had told her to, if for whatever reason she found herself in grave difficulty. At the time she had never revealed why, she'd just given her a secretive look and a knowing nod that Kristina hadn't been able to fathom out. With a smile and a shrug, she'd promised to do that just to please her - then had forgotten all about it until now.

Two - quite simply, she was now in really deep shit and actually had nowhere else to go. Well, nowhere that she could think of that was safe. It seemed as if these people Cox had told her about even had their moles on the main switchboards of most of the police forces in England. Otherwise, how come the sirens, when she'd demanded total silence?

She glanced quickly in the mirror again. Still nothing behind her and, she heaved a sigh, nothing in front of her only emptiness. Not long now before she reached the turn off, only a matter of minutes. The sooner she was off this open road the better. She would feel much calmer when she was safely on the island. In the morning she'd contact her superior, see what he had to say.

Anyhow, I'm probably worrying for nothing.

'Jesus.' She thumped the steering wheel. 'I've gone and panicked for nothing jumping to conclusions and now they'll be worrying about me. The switchboard mustn't have passed the message on, that's all, and with everything Cox said, I've got the whole police force in the nod with the families. Shit!'

She stared at the dark road in front of her, thinking, but still it's all very suspicious.

No, it's me. I've added one and one and come up with three.

She saw the car's headlights coming towards her as it rose over a sudden dip in the road and panicked again.

Please don't let it be them, she thought, gritting her teeth, as her heartbeat started to race.

Please not now.

Not when I'm so close to the Island.

But thankfully the car sped past her, doing well over the speed limit, and she heaved a sigh of relief. A few minutes later the sign for Holy island appeared. Taking a deep breath, and thanking God she'd made it this far, she slowed down to turn left when she spotted a car coming up behind her in the rear view mirror.

'Friggin' hell!' she muttered.

The car passed her as she took the turning and, once more thanking God, she sped quickly through the village of Beal and was soon approaching the causeway.

Her heart sank. Was that water covering the ground in front of her? 'Only one way to find out.' Stopping the car, she jumped out.

'Oh God, please, no, don't let it be flooded!' She moved forward, and her heart reached her feet. Bitterly disappointed, she stared at the water. The causeway was covered.

How deep though?

Please let it be passable.

Hesitatingly, she slipped her shoe off and put her right foot in. 'Not even ankle deep,' she muttered, watching the water swirl over her toes. Breathing a sigh of relief, and deciding to risk it, she quickly shook the sea water off her foot and put her shoe back on, then got back into the car.

Knowing she didn't have much time, because the causeway was very long, and the North Sea very unforgiving of fools who took chances, she started the car.

At first the car rolled along smoothly and she felt no resistance, so she slightly increased her speed, staring all the time at the rising water. People had been trapped before by not checking the crossing times. Quite frequently actually. It was always in the papers about people having to be rescued from the roof of their cars. She sincerely hoped she was not going to be one of them.

Who knows who will turn up to rescue me?

Who knows who I can trust?

'Stop it, just chill,' she muttered. 'No point in working myself up into a lather over something that might not happen.'

It's a calm night, so the weather's on my side. Should be easy. No problem. What the hell am I worried about? she was thinking, as she passed the refuge, a wooden hut on stilts made for people trapped in their cars, Mike had told her that the night he got stranded, the sea came up to the top step which was above the roof of his car. She prayed she wouldn't have to use it.

It was only a few minutes later, though, when she felt the car starting to drag. Her heart rate increased again, and she looked wildly around for help, even though she knew that there was no one there. She was on her own with no one to rely on, and real actual help would be a long time coming.

Stupid bloody idiot that I am.

I never should have tried it.

Me against the flaming North Sea.

'As if!' she muttered, her heartbeat once more quickening as she started to panic.

Terrified in case she had condemned herself to a watery grave, she pressed the pedal and breathed a bit easier when the car gained a small bit of traction. It gave a sudden lurch, then surged forward. She switched the wipers on and they swished back and forth, at first leaving a few streaks, but the spray soon took care of that.

'Keep moving...keep moving,' she muttered.

Careful, though. Agitatedly, she kept tapping the finger of her right hand on the steering wheel.

Slow, slow, keep it slow.

Too much and it might stall.

Just chill and take it steady, she told herself, knowing that she was well past the halfway stage now. It will all be over soon, dry land ahoy and all that.

But staring ahead of her as the waves grew bigger, she knew that, for all her bravado, this was it. There was no turning back.

CHAPTER THIRTEEN

The sound of sirens woke Danny Wilson up out of a deep sleep. He opened his eyes and blinked. 'What the?' he muttered, as he realised the sound assaulting his ears from all sides was not only that of sirens, but of deep heavy snoring. Old men snoring.

And lots of them!

He groaned.

'Where the fuck?'

'You're in hospital, mate,' a voice close to him said.

Danny got a shock when he heard the voice and quickly swung his head to the right, then felt immediately sick. 'Ohhh,' he groaned.

'You've been doing plenty of that an' all,' the old man said.

'Plenty of what?'

'Moaning and groaning. Been going on for hours, it has.'

Suddenly, Danny shot up. Ignoring the dizziness as best he could, he slid out of bed and stepped closer to the old man. 'Have they been in?' he whispered.

'Who?' the old man whispered back.

'Them!'

'Who's them?'

Danny starred at him. 'You taking the piss, or what?'

'No, I thought you was.'

Just then a young brown-haired nurse, with the largest green eyes Danny had ever seen, came into the ward. Going over to Danny's bed, she said, 'Let's have you back into bed. You know that you really should be resting.'

Warily, Danny let her help him back into bed, wondering if she was one of them.

'Where am I?' he asked.

'In hospital. Now go back to sleep. It's the middle of the night, and there are other patients to consider.'

I know I'm in a fucking hospital, he wanted to yell, but where, which hospital?

The nurse left the ward, and Danny turned back to the old man. 'Is she one of them?'

'One of who?'

'The fucking frenemy.'

'What's a fucking frenemy?'

'One of them, them who pretend to be your friend, but really the lying, back-stabbing bastards are your enemy.'

The old man thought it over. After a moment, he scratched his chin and said, 'Oh. One of them. I think you better go to sleep, son. Don't worry, I'll keep me eye out for the frenemy.'

'Will you?'

'Oh, aye.'

Danny heaved a sigh of relief. At long last, a friend.

As soon as his head hit the pillow, he was fast asleep, to dreams of them. Whichever way he turned, they were there.

He did not hear the old man nearly choke with laughing.

NORWICH

CHAPTER FOURTEEN

'So tell me,' Agent Josh Millar said to Tony Driver, 'what the fuck do the elite bastards want us to do for them now?'

Millar was tall, dark-skinned and handsome, and he knew it. He had a fancy for black suits and crisp white shirts. Vain though he was, he was a good man. Tonight he had been on the door and, feet apart with his hands behind his back, he had watched as, the meeting finally over, most of the families were either wandering into the bar to continue whatever petty grievances they had, or storming up the stairs to bed.

He'd been recruited into the agency seven years ago by Tony, and spent the first six months in permanent shock as things were slowly revealed to him. Five weeks ago, he'd found the agency within the agency, and thank God for that. He didn't know that Tony had been watching him for years, and had told him about the inner agency just before he reached melting point. It was what had saved his life.

Tony knew a good man when he saw one. He had also decided it was time that Josh was brought fully into the loop. They needed all the good men fully on board. Unknown to Josh though, that was the real reason for this conversation.

'Shall we have a stroll round the garden?' Without waiting for Josh to say yes or no, Tony headed towards the French doors. Knowing an order when he got one, Josh followed him and stood discreetly by when Tony spoke to a few family members on the way.

'Basically, what it boils down to is...' Tony shrugged. They reached the rose garden. 'As you heard in there...cutting the world population down. They've actually bought into their own hype about global warming.'

'But they started the rumour themselves.'

'Yep just one of their many ploys, that wasn't really thought out back then. Something for them to fall back on, and boy, have they fallen back on it big time.'

'Haven't the people suffered enough? Generations of secret family rule, and what do we have? Starving people and kids living in squalor all over the world, mostly in countries that have their own wealth but are ruled by a family member. Surely it would have been easier to stop all this centuries ago.'

'Think about it Josh. Realise just how easy it was to not stop it. Countries were separated from each other for a long, long time. Your ordinary man in the street didn't know what was going on half a mile away, never mind across the world.'

Josh nodded. 'I suppose.'

'They had plenty of time to dig their feet in and carve their ways on the rest of us. What do you think was the real reason behind the

Roman push around the world? The families were behind it - that, and just about every invasion since. And a few before then. Ordinary people, or 'peasants', as they like to call them...us...have no desires on anyone's property in the next county, never mind country. Why would they? Too busy feeding their own flaming family. But they are, and always have been, made to go to war, time and time again. All in the name of greed and power. Think how much the arms dealers make, all of them family owned. And there are wars going on in corners of the world most of the people haven't even heard of. Think about the pharmaceutical companies, inventing drug after drug, one to make you better from some unknown disease and yet another to make you better from the first drug. Again, all family owned, and on and on. As well as the street drugs, let's not forget them, mostly spin offs from the pharmaceutical companies.'

Josh blinked. This was a long speech from Tony, but as usual it all made sense.

'Look around you. This is not how it was meant to be. A few living in luxury, while most have nothing. Scrabbling a living from wherever they can. And now they are about to heap more injustice and cruelty on an unsuspecting world.'

'As well as breeding ignorance.'

Inwardly Tony groaned. He liked Millar, everyone did, but before he'd been recruited Millar had been a librarian. It was still hard to catch him without a book in his hand. He had been outraged at the library cuts, claiming that in a few years there would be no libraries at all, and so the families would be breeding exactly what they wanted. No books to read, no way to learn what was beyond their own village. And once the internet was shut down, and Kindles became obsolete, end of story, They would be truly back in the dark ages.

He hadn't known just how right he was. The e-book was part of a plan. In a few years, no more paper books that lasted for years, no more libraries left, and then the death of e-books. It was exactly what the families wanted, what had been planned.

First thing to go would be the internet, he was fond of saying, because it had sprung up so unexpectedly and caught everyone by surprise. Agents were already working on a virus that would wipe out all computers forever - except agents' computers, because they needed them to spy on everyone. Mobile phones were on the list, but it would be a while before they disappeared. Basically, what the families wanted was everyone back in the fifteenth century.

But first the human virus?

As if reading his mind, Josh asked, 'So is everything already in place to stop them?'

Tony looked at him and nodded. ' Don't worry its all in hand.'

'Clever of them to use England as the main source, though. I mean, London will be one of the most crowded cities on the planet shortly.'

'Yes, with the Olympics going on and people from all over the world in one place at the same time, it made a lot of sense. Put the nosocomial Legionnaires virus in the water, the most deadly strain of the disease, add a little extra to it, even though it already has a 30 per cent fatality rate, and bingo - millions of people infected and ready to take it home, right across Britain and the world. Why do you think you were inoculated a month ago?'

Josh shrugged, 'Thought it was just the ordinary flu jab.'

'You were supposed to think that.'

Josh nodded. 'So what's my job?'

'You're to stay here. We need faces that they recognise about the place, in case they become suspicious.'

'Can't we just blow the bastards up while we have them en masse?'

'But we haven't, have we? What we have here are mostly families, the deluded fools who think they're still in charge.'

'So why haven't the agents got rid of them? It makes sense.'

'Because a good portion of the agents are family-loyal, and it helps to have a scapegoat if word finally gets out that most of the human race have been slaves for centuries. Imagine what would happen.'

'Phew, the mind boggles. They would need to invent a new name for chaos.' Josh bent down and carefully snapped off a snow-white rose. After smelling its perfume, he placed it in his lapel.

'Exactly,' Tony said, when he had Josh's full attention again.

'It's still hard to take in that they've gotten away with it for so long.'

'Have they, though?'

Josh raised his eyebrows. Hmm. This is interesting, he thought.

But just then Tony's phone rang, Taking it out of his pocket, he looked at caller ID and said, 'I've got to take this call, OK? We'll talk some more later.' With a nod he turned and, phone to his ear, walked deeper into the garden, leaving Josh desperate to know the rest of the history of the lives he'd become entangled with.

NORTHUMBERLAND

CHAPTER FIFTEEN

Gripping the wheel tightly, Kristina ploughed on. She jumped slightly when spray started hitting the side windows with force, praying that it wasn't anywhere near the engine. She stared intently in front of her, actually picturing herself battling to swim in the rough sea. A good swimmer she was not, a couple of lengths was about the best she could manage without stopping for a rest. Against these crashing waves she wouldn't stand a chance.

With the windscreen wipers on full, she tried to push the images out of her mind as the car gamely moved forward. She tried hard to push the thought away that she was in a situation which made her totally helpless.

Suddenly, she gasped out loud. Is that the end of the causeway coming up?

'Oh, please God,' she muttered. 'I'm gonna make it.'

Excitement flooded through her veins as suddenly, with no warning, she was clear. The car, free of the restraints of the powerful sea, jumped forward. Kristina slammed on the brakes, but the car just kept on gathering speed. In seconds she went from elation to horror.

Heart firmly in her mouth, she rammed the car into second gear and pumped madly on the brake.

At last, after what seemed forever and at breakneck speed, she felt the brakes grip and the car begin to slow down. Trembling, Kristina heaved a sigh of relief as, regaining control, she drove past the car park and down the main street. Turning left, and again left into Sandham Lane, she came to a stop outside Aunt May's cottage.

For a moment, she hugged the wheel. Taking deep breaths to calm herself, and knowing just how lucky she had been, she slipped out of the car and carefully, still trying to be as quiet as she could, closed the door. Noticing how far up the water had come, she shook her head in disbelief. No wonder the brakes wouldn't work properly.

Jesus!

She would never be so lucky again.

Going up the path, she could smell Aunt May's clematis. For a moment it felt as if a little bit of Aunt May was watching over her. She knocked on the door, waited a moment before knocking again although her instinct seemed to be telling her the house was empty.

'Where are you Aunt May?' she muttered.

Bending down, and with a bit of a struggle, she moved the third plant pot from the right, which was full of purple pansies. Underneath was the front door key.

A minute later she was inside and heading for the kitchen. She desperately needed a cup of tea, before she sat down and analysed everything that had happened in the last hour.

While the kettle boiled, and with shaking hands, knowing she was close to exhaustion, she tried to get out of her mind the picture of the man's thumb landing at his feet, shaking her head in amazement at the thought. That sort of thing you could never plan in a lifetime!

Thanks Grandma! she thought, as yet another picture of her grandmother sharpening the blade entered her mind.

'About time an' all,' she sighed a moment later, smacking her lips in anticipation as she dropped a tea bag into a pink mug covered with tiny white daisies. She poured the water in and found the sugar in the top cupboard. Knowing, by the way her hand was still shaking, that she was probably in shock, she put three teaspoons in the mug, and a dash of milk. Then she went through into the sitting room, thinking, at last - a flaming cup of tea.

Switching the light on with her elbow as she passed the switch, she looked around. Nothing at all had changed since that last time she had been in here. There were flowers everywhere. She smiled, remembering the first time she'd met Aunt May. It had been winter, but she had smelled of flowers, and the house had been full of them. With a sigh, Kristina sat down.

She had been staring down at the carpet. When she looked up, and halfway through the cup of tea she had been dying for, for what seemed like ages now, she saw an envelope on the mantelpiece that she hadn't noticed before, propped up against one of Aunt May's ornaments. The scrawl on the front looked like her name. Squinting, she tried to make it out, but in the end had to get up.

It was addressed to her. Puzzled, she quickly tore it open. Inside there was a single sheet of paper, with ten words on it.

'Go and visit an old friend with a beard. NOW.' The final word had been heavily inked in.

'What the...?' It was the capitals that worried her. And what old friend with a beard?

Jesus, Aunt May!

NORWICH

CHAPTER SIXTEEN

Fools, nothing but fools, the whole fucking lot of them, Tarasov thought, as he entered the lift and angrily slapped the number that would take him to his floor.

Got a good mind to go home and leave them to it!

He knew, though, that was something he could not do. He had to keep the pretence up a little longer. Make too many waves and the whole barbaric lot would turn on him, and all would be lost.

Lovilla, even though he had half expected it - scratch that, even though he'd known it - had been a big disappointment. Just like her mother had. She'd thrown her lot in with the fools who thought things could go on like they had centuries ago. He would deal with her later. One way or another he would make her see her mistake. But the fool he called son!

By the time the lift stopped, his fury had built to an all-time high. With clenched fists, he stormed along the corridor. As he was passing another lift, the doors opened and a young woman pushed a trolley full of clean towels into the corridor, just missing him.

Ella's heart jumped into her throat when she realised who she had nearly pushed the trolley into.

Oh my God. She froze for a moment, Please just let him walk on past… please God.

Tarasov glared at Ella and snapped, 'Clumsy, clumsy fool! I'll not forget this. Thank your lucky stars, peasant, I've got other things on my mind.'

As Ella stared after him, her heart still pounding, he carried on down the corridor, pausing for a moment outside a door close to his. He touched the 'Do Not Disturb' sign, before turning back to Ella, who swallowed hard.

'Make sure this sign is observed, or it's you I'll be looking for, understand?'

She nodded and uttered a meek, 'Yes, sir,' although inside she was seething and wanted nothing more than to actually kill him.

So what or who the hell is in there? she thought, as she knocked discreetly on number ten, who had asked for fresh towels for the third time today. The door was opened by a scowling young woman with long black hair and a matching black eye, who held out her hands for the towels.

Ella placed a matching pair of powder blue bath towels into the waiting hands, wanting to say, 'There's help nearby if you want it', but knowing that could quite easily jeopardise everything. Sometimes these women, little more than slaves, had been so brainwashed that they would go running to their masters at the slightest whisper of someone against them. She had seen it again and again. Hadn't she been in the same position herself? That was, until she woke up and realised that there was a different life, and if she couldn't live it, well, better be dead than the life she was living. She'd heard the rumour, taken the chance, and here she was.

Fighting back!

I'll keep my eye on her, see how it plays out. For now I need to get back downstairs and let Coral know about the locked room, as well as the grand master plan that was brewing.

Quickly she handed the towels over and made her way back to the lift, noting the door number before she left. She would keep her eye on the goings on in there, in case there was the slightest hint that the woman could be rescued.

Back downstairs, she said she was nipping out for a smoke before knocking off time. They weren't allowed to smoke in the hotel. That pleasure was for families only. Figuring themselves above the law, they smoked wherever they wanted to. Once outside, she wandered over to the old wishing well, carefully looking around to make sure she wasn't being observed, but knowing the need to be very careful. Just because she couldn't see anyone didn't mean that there wasn't someone there watching. She dropped her lighter on the far side, away from the windows. Pretending to search for it, she prised a brick loose and pulled out a mobile phone. Quickly she dialled a number and, still on her hands and knees, put the phone to her ear.

Within moments it was answered by Coral. Ella quickly told her of the locked room. The rest she would tell her when she got back, there was no time now.

'Hmm, interesting. It could of course be full of fresh slaves,' Coral said. 'Do what you can to find out without putting yourself in danger. Your post there is too important to lose.'

'Will do.' Ella switched off immediately. The less time on the phone, the harder it was to trace.

With the phone tucked in her sleeve, and smoking her cigarette, she walked a further fifty yards and stubbed her cigarette out on an old tree trunk, dropping the phone into a hole in the trunk, knowing that it was too dark for anyone from the hotel to see at this distance. She pushed the piece of loose bark back over the hole and, hands in her pockets, casually sauntered back to the hotel.

CHAPTER SEVENTEEN

The sun was just starting its long crawl up a pale pink sky as Aunt May walked down the path, with Brother David close behind and towering above her. It had been a long night, nearly a six-hour drive from Seahouses in Northumberland to this quiet, unassuming back street in Norwich.

Just before Aunt May reached the door, and as Brother David was stifling a yawn, the door opened. Aunt May was at once engulfed in a hug by a young woman whose large hazel eyes sparkled as she met Brother David's eyes over Aunt May's shoulder.

Her smile was so dazzling that, slightly confused by it, Brother David stepped back.

'It's so good to see you, Aunt May.'

'And you too, my lovely Coral.'

Coral turned to Brother David. 'And you must be big Mike. Wow, you never told me he was so gorgeous, Aunt May.'

The next minute she had her arms wrapped around Brother David, and planted a kiss firmly on his mouth. Leaning back, she looked into his eyes and winked.

'Erm… I think you've put your bloody foot in it again, my dear,' Aunt May laughed, and went on, 'Bloody hell, Coral. This isn't Mike, this is David. Brother David. He's a monk.'

'What! Oh, my God.' Coral backed off. It was hard to tell who had the reddest face, her or Brother David, as she went on, 'I'm so sorry, so sorry. I mean, you don't look like any monk I've ever met.' She looked him up and down. 'Not that I've met many, that is.'

'It, it's fine…really, no harm done.' Brother David held his hand out. He tried his best to ignore the delicious tingle he felt as they shook hands. With his other hand, just for something to do with it, he nervously fingered his jacket, as he went on, 'You, er... you weren't to know, um…were you.'

'OK, again, I'm sorry. It, er... it won't happen again.' This time Coral laughed, and pulled a face at Aunt May who was still grinning. 'Kettles on, beds are ready. You will be wanting sleep, won't you? Gotta be shattered after the drive down.'

'I'm fine, napped nearly all the way, but Brother David drove most of the bloody night. I suspect he'll need some shuteye.' Aunt May raised her eyebrows as she looked at Brother David.

Still slightly embarrassed, Brother David nodded. 'I'll skip the tea, if you don't mind.'

'No bother,' Coral said.

By this time they were inside the house, and passing the door to the garden. 'Your bedroom, Brother David, is upstairs, the first door on your right.' Coral pointed up the stairs.

Brother David nodded and made for the stairs. He could hear her giggling to Aunt May, who was shushing her with a smile in her voice, as he reached the room. Quickly he opened the door and went in. The bed was a very welcoming sight.

Stripping his clothes off as he walked the half-dozen steps to the bed, he gratefully sank onto the comfortable mattress, and sighed. After a few minutes he turned over, praying for the sleep that, even though he was exhausted, was evading him.

He flopped onto his back for a few minutes, then onto his right side, then, with a big sigh, heaved his body back over to the other side. No good. He knew the reason why he couldn't sleep. The image of the girl and the kiss would not leave his mind.

It had been a long time since he'd felt like this, in fact just before he'd joined the monastery. He closed his eyes, squeezing them tightly. Remembering one summer's night after a local teenage party, and a particularly pretty blonde girl, he began to pray.

Downstairs Aunt May was sipping tea, with her feet up on a small red leather stool.

'Bloody well needed that all right.' She took another sip, then smacked her lips and said, 'Come on then, Coral, fill me in.'

'Right, sorry about the mix up.' She grinned. 'But the last news was Mike Yorke had gone AWOL. I assumed when you walked in with the brother in normal everyday clothes that you'd found him. I mean, he is dishy, isn't he? What the hell did a gorgeous bloke like him want to become a monk for?'

'Well, for question one, I do have. a good idea where Mike Yorke is being held.'

'Oh?'

'Not very far from here, actually.'

'Let me guess.'

'You already have. You see, Mike's biological father is one of the families.'

'No way!'

Aunt May nodded. 'Yes. And as to question two, why the dishy Dave became a monk...' She shrugged. 'I have no idea. It sort of happened overnight. Why? You'll have to ask him. So, a question for you now - who do we have slaving away in the Hotel California?'

Coral smiled. 'You got that right, you can check in but you can never leave.'

Coral's phone rang before she could answer Aunt May. She took the phone out of her pocket, looked at it and said, 'Gotta take this, Aunt May. It's Ella.'

Aunt May nodded.

A minute later, she put the phone away and looked at Aunt May. 'That was Ella. She's down at the hotel, and she reckons there's a locked room. Mike Yorke, do you think?'

'Definitely.'

Upstairs, Brother David, his faith sorely tested, continued to toss and turn.

CHAPTER EIGHTEEN

Detective Inspector Mike Yorke held the gun and, slowly pointing it straight ahead, squeezed the trigger. Once, twice, three times he fired, but no one fell - well, no one that he could see in the thick fog that surrounded him. Slowly, his legs feeling as if he was struggling his way through waist-high mud, he moved forward towards the light. With each step, it grew brighter. He stepped through the last tendrils of fog, blinked, and opened his eyes to bright sunlight. He blinked again twice, then looked around.

No bodies, just a dream, he thought with relief, drawing air into his lungs then exhaling loudly.

'Wherever the hell I am,' he muttered a moment later, shaking his head, 'I hope I'm not fucking paying for it.'

His eyes scoured the opulence of the room, from the thick red velvet curtains, the red carpet, which looked like he would sink in ankle deep if he was to stand on it, the real gold trimmings on the cream furniture, and finally resting on the gold back-to-back unicorns on the ceiling, which looked both solid and real gold. He finally gave into his thoughts, and the fact he'd been trying to dodge, that his right hand was handcuffed to the headboard.

He slumped, as everything that had happened last night flooded his mind. 'No way,' he muttered. 'No fucking way is that bastard my father. Impossible!'

There's gotta be a mistake.

Fucking hell.

He gave his arm a shake, and his heart sank further when he heard the rattle of metal on metal. Pulling himself up the bed until he was eye level with the cuffs, and seeing no way at all to free himself, he let his head fall back on the headboard and stared at the ceiling in deep despair.

His memory coming back, he remembered every punch, slap and kick he'd received yesterday.

So, he reasoned with a sinking heart, if he's my father, then the twat who did this has got to be my brother.

No fucking way. Talk about the family from hell!

'Or half-brother,' he muttered. Looking down at his naked body, he expected to find a whole mess of bruising, but was surprised to see what looked like only shadows of bruises. He'd always had good healing skin, but this looked like he'd had the shit kicked out of him four or five days ago, not last night.

Unless… no, it was last night!

So what the hell have they been pumping into me?

Just proves another point Cox raised, the bastards have a cure for everything that the ordinary bloke doesn't know about. Bet they live a lot longer and illness free as well.

And some fucking brother!

But we'll meet again, bro, hopefully without the fucking hand-cuffs, and God help you.

Too much water under the bridge to feel any emotion towards a family he'd never known existed till now, and too much information to take in properly.

He stretched, luxuriated for a moment, before giving a sudden vicious yank on the handcuffs, which did nothing but make his wrist hurt. 'Fucking hell,' he muttered. 'How the hell am I gonna get out of this?'

Turning on his right side, he reached his left hand up and felt the cuffs. No way, far too flaming tight. He felt along the bed frame, looking for a weak spot, pulling the cuffs as he moved his hand along, but it all seemed pretty solid.

'Shit.' He gave another yank on the cuffs.

No way out of this, mate. He moved sideways along the bed in the other direction, but still failed to find a weak spot in the frame. That was when he spotted the glass of water on the bedside cabinet. The water was just within his reach, but further along, right at the very end of the cabinet, was a key. And this was totally out of reach.

'Tormenting twats!' he muttered.

He looked down at his naked body again, and shrugged. If they think keeping me clothes-less will stop me getting outta here... big mistake. 'Bastards.'

He sighed. Really, this whole friggin' predicament is nothing short of surreal.

But wasn't everything these days? His eyes had been opened to a different world, one that co-existed with his own, and had done for many centuries.

Who else knows?

And just exactly how many families are involved?

The information he had been given was patchy, but the blanks had not been to hard to fill in, because so much of what he'd been told definitely added up.

How to put it right, though!

His plan had been to go after the top guys. No point in taking the legs out - this had to be done from the top. And if Tony--

What the fuck am I thinking about? IF?

He's involved right up to his armpits.

The bastard.

And what about Aunt May?

Surely not.

Weird though that Tony's involved, and Aunt May seems to know a lot of things.

She wouldn't!

Dave?

No way…but maybe's that's why he turned into a monk, too much for him to handle…No, he wouldn't have been able to keep it from me, and Aunt May wouldn't be involved in anything shady.

What the hell am I thinking?

Angrily, he yanked again on the cuffs, with as much success as he'd had the last time. He wanted to scream and yell, bang his feet up and down on the bed, but deep inside he knew it was pointless. All he could do was go along, and hopefully fight his way out of it once they unchained him.

Suppose they kill me, it's better than this!

And you can guarantee I'll take more than one of the bastards down with me.

NORTHUMBERLAND

CHAPTER NINETEEN

Around about the time that Mike Yorke opened his eyes, Danny once again opened his, only to much less extravagant surroundings, and having no recollection of waking up frequently through the night. Like Mike Yorke, he stared around in complete puzzlement for a moment, wondering where he was.

Then he realised again. It's a friggin' hospital!

Jesus Christ.

How?

What the hell happened?

He looked to his right. An old man, with a bald head with as many wrinkles as a turkey has on its neck, and nearly as red, sat on the edge of the next bed staring at him.

'You all right, mate?' the old man asked. Then, without giving Danny a chance to answer, he went on, 'I'm surprised you haven't woken up in a straightjacket in the nutter ward, to tell you the truth, the way you were flaming well carrying on last night. Oh aye, and not a frenemy in sight.' He grinned at Danny, showing a toothless mouth.

'What?'

'What? you say? I'm telling you, mate, not a single flaming soul has had a wink of sleep all friggin' night, in fact at one point we was wishing "them", whoever they flaming well are, would come and get you.' He looked around the ward at the sleeping old men. 'Well, us that were awake, that is.'

'Sorry,' Danny muttered, before groaning, and flopping his head back on to the pillow.

The man shrugged. 'Guess we've all been in that state a few times, son. But a bit of advice - don't, whatever you do, mention "them" again, whoever the hell they are, to the docs or anyone else. 'Cos they'll have you outta here and in the nut ward in a flash.'

Danny stared unblinkingly at the man. He had nothing to say, and knew it. No one would believe him anyhow.

A few moments later a tall male nurse, with blond spiked hair tipped with red, was at his bedside.

Looking up at him, Danny muttered, 'What happened?'

The nurse smiled and said, 'Oh dear, you tell me, love. I only know that we had to pump your stomach, my love. Well, not me exactly, the doctors, you know, and I wasn't on duty anyway…But because you were in serious danger of suffering alcohol poisoning, they had to do it. And trust me, love, you don't want that, it's damn awful.' He shivered, emphasizing just how damn awful alcoholic poisoning is.

Danny took a moment to think this through. His question had been about the blood-red tips on the nurse's hair, only the daft sod hadn't got it. Then he said. 'When can I get outta here?'

'The doctor will be round at ten o' clock, my love. Rest assured he'll let you know when you can go.'

'Well, how soddin' long do they usually keep people in for? For that sort of thing?'

'It depends, my love.'

'On what?'

'Doctor will want to do some tests.'

Danny felt like screaming. It was like talking to a fucking machine that was obsessed with love.

'OK, let's get this straight. One, I'm not, nor ever will be, your love. Two, so just get my clothes now, will you? Three, 'cos I'm outta here. Like right now.'

The nurse tutted and gave an exaggerated shrug. 'Sorry, no can do, my--'

'I've said I'm off, OK? Feeling fine. And you ain't the coppers, so you can't keep me here if I don't want to stay. So for fuck's sake, where the hell's me gear?'

'I'm sorry, but your clothes were in no fit state to be worn. They've been incinerated. You'll have to get a family member to bring some fresh ones in.'

'For fuck's sake.'

The nurse frowned down at him. 'Please, sir, be respectful of all our other patients.'

Danny glanced over at the old man, and guessed rightly that he was doing his best not to piss himself laughing - even though his sniggers were getting louder. He gave him the same frown the nurse was raining down on him.

He spun his head back to the nurse. 'So when's the fucking doctor coming in, then?'

'An hour or so, probably, though he may be running late.'

'He's always running late,' the old man put in.

Throwing him a glare, the nurse turned back to Danny. 'Would you like some light breakfast now? We have some lovely cornflakes this morning,' he smiled. 'Toast, strawberry jam, or perhaps there may be some very nice scrambled eggs?'

'An hour? A fucking hour?' Danny almost shouted. He swung his legs out of the bed. 'No way, mate, am I hanging around for an hour, never mind the "so". I know how long "so's" take. And you know what you can do with your fucking very nice scrambled eggs.'

'Please, you're disturbing the other patients.'

'And the lovely cornflakes, and the other stuff you said. 'Cos there ain't no argument... I'm off. Gone. Have a good life. In fact, you'll run now, if you know what's good for you.'

'Please, sir, the patients.'

'What patients?' Danny waved his arm, taking in the fifteen bed ward. Every bed was taken up with sleeping old men.

'You couldn't disturb this lot if you tried to, you bloody fool. They wouldn't hear a fucking brass band in full swing marching through this fucking dump. They're all in the knackers yard, fucking waiting for God. What the fuck am I doing in here amongst this lot, anyhow? I'm hardly drawing me pension.'

'It was the only available bed. And if you don't get back into bed, I'm calling security.'

'Yeah, well, call them. Go on, I dare you. And before they get here, tell them I said to fuck right off.'

The nurse pursed his lips and flounced off out of the ward. Danny turned to the old man, who was now purple.

'Best friggin' entertainment I've had in a month, mate,' he said before, unable to control it any longer, he burst out laughing, and alternatively gasping for air.

'You got any clothes I can borrow?' Danny asked him. 'I've really got to get outta here, like five minutes ago.'

'Hmm…I have, though I doubt very much if they'll fit you, bonny lad,' he wheezed.

'Whatever. I really need to be gone.'

'Why? In case "them" come looking for you? Sorry, couldn't resist it.' He laughed again. 'Here, son,' he pointed to his locker, 'take whatever you want.'

Danny gritted his teeth and moved quickly to the old man's locker. In moments he was dressed in a pair of dark grey trousers, two sizes too small for him, and a dark brown cardigan with holes in the sleeves, and one pocket hanging on by a few threads, which smelled strongly of a mixture of pipe smoke and wet dog.

'You haven't got--'

The old man held out a ten pound note before Danny could finish what he was going to say.

Gratefully, Danny snatched the tenner. 'Thanks, mate. I'll get it back to you, that's a promise.'

'Don't worry, son, seems you've got enough problems. And trust me, it was worth it for the entertainment value. Beats betting on two raindrops on the window in this morgue.'

Danny looked around the ward and pictured a bunch of old men staring at the window, gambling on which raindrop would hit the bottom first, and shuddered.

'Thanks again.'

'OK. Now get going. Turn left through the door and then first right. That'll bring you out the back way, 'cos the security guards will no doubt be on their way here. Trust me, Nurse Soft Shite will have gone for them.'

'OK, and thanks again.'

'Get out of here, will you? And be careful. Some of your babbling last night made sense.'

For a moment Danny stared in amazement at the old man. 'You believe me?'

'You don't get to my age and live through two world wars without hearing a thing or two that ain't your regular run of the mill stuff. I remember one time in the trenches...' For a moment, his eyes glazed over. Then he sighed and went on, 'Never mind, bonny lad. But a bit of advice. Always keep an open mind, that's my motto. A closed mind learns nowt… Now get the hell outta here.'

'I'm gone.'

'OK, son. Careful you don't burst outta them trousers, mind you.' He laughed loudly again.

Danny took off at a run, and turned the corner just as the security guards arrived. He reached the exit and looked quickly both ways. As he stepped through the door, he spotted a bus just outside of the wall, which was only a few metres away, but easily well over two metres tall. Although his instinct was to go for the wall, he knew he'd never be able to scale it in these pants. He ran for the steps he'd spotted to his right and took them two at a time, but he was too late to catch the bus. It pulled away as he jumped over the last step.

'Damn.' He shoved his hands into his pockets, wondering when the next bus was due. He sincerely hoped it came well before the black clouds over to the east arrived.

Leaning against the bus-stop pole, he watched an old woman in a red coat cross the road.

'Looks like it's gonna rain again.' She smiled at him as she stepped inside the shelter.

What's with the fucking weather? Danny thought. Jesus! You can practically guarantee that a perfect fucking stranger will make some comment about it, for fuck's sake!

'It's gonna piss down,' he snapped, staring at her.

She shrugged, taking no notice of his angry tone. 'Probably. You can smell it in the air, can't you. We've had more rain this year than

I've ever known. But then you've had a lot of rain in your life recently, haven't you?'

'What?' Danny was taken aback. Talking about the weather with a stranger was one thing, but personal stuff? No way. Anyhow, how does she know what's been going on, unless she's one of...Them. Oh God, she must be.

'Never mind. Here, Danny.' She held out her hand.

Danny stared at the brown envelope she was holding as if it was going to grow teeth and bite him. Then it suddenly dawned on him that she knew his name. He shivered, feeling cold all over.

She is one of them...Gotta be.

Gotta get away from here, he thought, starting to panic as he looked wildly from side to side, and shaking inside as he wondered which way to run.

'Danny.'

'What?' He paused a moment and stared at her.

'Take it. Trust me, it's from a friend.' She held the envelope out again. 'Take it.'

'Why should I trust you?' He stepped quickly back.

'I don't blame you, after all that's happened lately. But if I said that I know Shelly, or rather some very good friends of mine know Shelly, would you please take it?'

He shook his head, looking even more suspiciously at her as he thought, Shelly... Shelly is to blame for all this... Don't you know that? Oh God, where is she?

'Shelly needs you, Danny, she really does. Without you, my friends don't think she'll make it.'

'She…you know where she is?'

And why wouldn't she know where Shelly is, for fuck's sake, she knows who I am. He shook his head in disbelief. This whole thing just gets weirder and weirder by the day.

The woman nodded. 'In the envelope is your passport and a plane ticket to Heathrow, where you'll be met and taken by car the rest of the way to Shelly in Norwich. In a few minutes, there'll be a car arriving here to take you to Newcastle airport.'

'No.' Danny waved his arms at her. 'Ain't getting on no plane, with no strangers, and deffo not getting into no fucking car, and that's a fact.' - remembering the last time he was in a car with strangers, and ended up in the monastery. 'Thanks, but no thanks.' He backed right to the end of the bus shelter.

Then a sudden thought struck him. How the fucking hell did you get my passport?

Ignoring his question, she went on, 'Danny, you're on your own out here, but you have to trust somebody. Please trust me when I tell you that Shelly really needs you.'

'You sure you're not one of them… I mean, how can I trust you? 'Cos you're gonna tell me a whole bunch of lies anyhow, aren't you…No, keep it.'

'Danny, Shelly is on suicide watch.'

'Suicide?' His mouth hung open. 'In Norwich?'

Patiently, the old woman went on, 'Yes, Danny. You really must go. There isn't much time until the families start looking for you, because they'll have contacts in the hospital. In fact, they're probably already here… Ah, here comes the car.'

Instead of looking at the car, which was pulling up alongside them, he said, 'You know about them, don't you? I mean, you really know they're real? All this isn't some crazy fucking dream I'm stuck in the middle of…I'm not going nuts, am I? Please tell me I'm not gonna end up in the fucking nut house forever.' He reached his hand imploringly towards her.

Thrusting the envelope into his hand, she said, 'Yes, Danny, it's all real, and you have no reason to doubt yourself. Trust me.'

Danny felt like laughing his head off. Trust you? Easy enough said, Mrs…but no way!

'You're mixed up in something so huge, they'll do their best to shut you up. Even though you're nothing more than an irritating piece of fly shit on a wall to them.'

'Nice.' Danny glared at her.

'Just get into the car, and go see Shelly.' She scuttled towards him and pushed him in the direction of the car.

'Get off me.' He batted his hands at her.

What the hell, he thought, who does she think she's pushing, the old bat. I'm pissed right off with being ordered around by every fucking body. Seems it's all day every day now.

'Danny, you have to go now. Trust me, there's no more time left.'

Convinced she was one of them, he said, holding his hands out in a placating gesture, 'OK, OK, I get it... I'll go.' His intention though was to run as far away from her as he could.

He looked towards the car. A large red Audi with blacked-out windows. He had no idea of who might be inside. Before he could move, the back door opened, cutting off his escape route. His heart gave a lurch.

Hesitating, he turned back to the woman. 'You sure it's not them? I mean, I don't even know you. You could easily be--'

The next moment, he was grabbed by a pair of strong arms and dragged into the car.

NORWICH

CHAPTER TWENTY

Ella hurried outside into the bike shed. Climbing onto her bike, she made for the exit hoping against hope that none of the guards were hanging about. There was a certain one who looked like he'd never seen a bath nor a barber for God knows how long, who had his eye on her, and if things went the way he seemed to be wanting them to, then her position here would be untenable. Even for the cause she would never go down that road ever again. To be truthful, though, it would never be expected of her.

But it would be bad for all. Her job here had been instrumental in teaching them so much about the enemy, and so much was drawing to a head that to put a new girl in her place would be more than dangerous. It could be disastrous.

Looking right then left, she turned on to the road and headed for Norwich. Most of the road was tree-lined, with fields behind the trees. It was very quiet, as usual. She met one oncoming car, and was only passed by two cars the whole four miles. Her heart was in her mouth as usual each time a car passed, in case somehow she'd been sussed out and they had come after her.

Reaching the street where the safe house was, she pedalled quickly down and into the back yard. Opening the back door, she walked in and found Coral in the kitchen.

'Phew,' she said, removing her helmet. 'I could really murder a cuppa, and I'm starving.'

'Kettle's still hot, love, and you can eat till your heart's content.' Coral replied, making her way into the sitting room with a plate piled high with biscuits.

'Who are those for?"

'Guess.'

'She's arrived?' Ella smiled.

'Yup, and you'll never guess what I did.'

On the way into the sitting room, down a long corridor with doors on each side, Coral told Ella about her practically jumping on Brother David.

'Wow, you surpassed yourself this time all right.' Ella grinned, picking one of the biscuits off the plate.

'Don't I know it.'

'Yeah, well, don't fret too much. He's a monk. I know he'll forgive you, it's his job.'

'Hello, Ella.' Smiling, Aunt May rose from her chair as Ella and Coral entered the room.

'Aunt May.' Ella hurried across the room and gave Aunt May a hug. 'How are you?'

'Fine, dear.' Aunt May sat back down, crossed her legs and put her hands over her knees. 'So what news from the hotel this morning, Ella?'

'Well.' Ella sat down facing Aunt May, while Coral sat in the seat next to her. 'The meeting last night went exactly as we thought it would. The arrogant bastards still think they have the right to control the rest of the world. Also, they are going to poison the water in London, in time for the Olympics and that's just for starters.'

'No change there, then,' Coral stated. 'They've been poisoning everyone since forever with their drugs.'

'Any against what they're planning?' Aunt May asked.

'Actually, there were a few objections, and the usual amount of rows, but they were all overruled.'

'It's what we bloody well expected. Any thing else that seemed out of focus?'

'Yes, there's a locked room on the top floor.'

Aunt May raised her eyebrows. She looked from one to the other. 'Hmm, so you said on the phone. I think Mike Yorke might just be in that bloody room. Our far-seers can't bloody well find him, perhaps they have their own seers masking the place…Any way you can safely get a key, Ella?'

'I can get my hands on the master key.'

'OK, what we need now is a plan of action.' Again she looked first at Coral, then at Ella.

Before anyone could say anything else, the door opened and Shelly walked in. At first she didn't notice Aunt May, who studied her with a slight frown on her face.

'Hi, Shelly.' Coral said. 'How yer feeling?'

Shelly shrugged. ' A bit better…I guess.'

'Well, here's Aunt May.' Coral pointed her finger over Shelly's shoulder.

Shelly turned and gave Aunt May a weak smile. Aunt May stood up and held out her arms. 'Come and sit with me, child. I've heard all about your ordeal.'

Wrapping the pink dressing gown tightly around her body, Shelly shuffled over to Aunt May. For a brief moment, she let the older woman hold her. Then, breaking contact before she burst into tears, she sat down on the seat next to Aunt May, who was now staring at a newspaper on the edge of the table that Coral had been unknowingly blocking from her view.

'What's that?' she asked.

All three girls looked in the direction that Aunt May had been staring at, before she walked over and picked the newspaper up.

The headlines read, FOURTH MISSING TEENAGER IN THREE DAYS.

They all looked at each other, the same thoughts running through their heads. Under the headlines were pictures of the four girls - all with long black hair.

'No,' Ella gasped. 'He's here…Well, that's all we fucking well need, isn't it, that twat in the equation.'

Shelly looked at them. 'Didn't you know?' Ella and Coral swung their heads to Aunt May in puzzlement.

Finishing the article, Aunt May looked up. 'I guessed as much. We placed him in the area.'

'You knew he was here and didn't say?' Coral's stare changed to one of disbelief.

'It wasn't definite, and I was going to tell you girls as soon as we knew for certain, but there hasn't been much chance. And we couldn't risk word getting out that we suspected where the bloody evil rat was. We followed him to Bradford, but sadly the two girls who were shadowing him were found out. And nothing's been heard from them since.'

She was silent for a moment, and Ella and Coral held their breath. Shelly, who had listened quietly, put in, 'He got them, didn't he.'

Aunt May nodded.

'Were they scourged?'

Aunt May sighed. 'Yes, Shelly, they were.'

'Oh, God.'

'Scourged, what's scourged?' Ella asked.

Coral shook her head. 'Trust me. You don't want to know.'

Ella folded her arms across her chest. 'Oh, I do so want to know.'

'My best friend Alicia was scourged,' Shelly said. Her voice was filled with a deep sadness as, taking a deep breath, she went on, 'A scourging consists of thirty-nine lashes with a wooden handled whip roughly eighteen inches long, with nine leather thongs about six to seven feet long. At the end of each thong is a piece of lead shot, and attached to the lead shot there are pieces of sheep or cattle bone. The lasher snaps his wrist a certain way, which causes the weight of the lead shot to dig into the flesh. The sheep bones dig deep in under the surface and pull small shards of skeletal muscle out of the body.'

'I'm gonna be sick.' Ella held her hand over her mouth. 'I knew we were dealing with sick bastards. The families are bad enough…But this, this bastard renegade? Well…he's something else.' She ran for the toilet.

The three women watched her go. Aunt May sighed. 'The Leader's antics have mostly been kept quiet. We are up against so much. The fool thinks he's living in the thirteenth century. Although the rest of the families have very little to do with him, and probably want him dead themselves, they would certainly protect him against us. It's the way they do things.'

'So what do we do now? Ella asked, coming back into the room with a determined look on her face. 'Seeing as there will definitely be more than four girls and boys missing. These,' she waved at the newspaper, 'are only the ones who get reported as missing.' She looked at Coral. 'Didn't you see the article when you got the paper?'

'No, sorry.'

'So what now?' Ella asked Aunt May.

'Now we have that talk, and I bring you both up to date.'

Shelly looked at Aunt May and frowned.

'Sorry. I meant you, too, Shelly. We honestly do need you.'

'I'll put the kettle on.' Ella stood up.

CHAPTER TWENTY-ONE

Grim-faced, the Leader paced about his new domain. Overnight the finishing touches had been put in place, and the large house had been transformed into a complete copy of the monastery near Holy Island. Out in the sheds, a group of young people picked up off the streets over the last few days with the promise of free drugs, free love, and anything else they wanted, were waking up to find themselves truly in hell.

Suddenly the Leader turned to face his two personal guards. He eyed the new one, a replacement for his regular Chinese guard who had died less than twenty-four hours ago.

His doctors had shaken their heads, and told him they could find no reason for the guard's sudden death. It was just one of those things. Sometimes even the super-fit can suffer a heart attack and die. Sometimes it isn't even a heart attack at all. Sometimes the body just shuts down, for no apparent reason.

Whatever, he thought, one guard is as good as another. Plenty of peasants to replace them.

Throwing back his head, he laughed, a wild maniacal sound that could be heard throughout the building, striking fear into the hearts of the confused teenagers just starting their first day of slavery.

'You,' he said to the new guard a moment later. 'Far too much face hair. Get rid of it right now.'

'Yes, my Leader.' He turned and left the room at once, heading for the stairs.

It meant nothing to the Leader that the dead guard had served him faithfully for over ten years. He was just a peasant, and therefore as expendable as all and any of them. More like a pet dog, really. And as such, totally expendable.

He turned to the other guard. 'When will production begin?' he demanded.

'Within the hour, my Leader,' the old guard replied.

'Good...Pick me one out and bring her now.' He turned and headed for his bedroom.

'Yes, my Leader.' He muttered under his breath, 'I know just the one you'll want.'

The new guard walked out of the room and into the corridor, ducking into the first doorway on his right. Quickly he closed the door behind him then, after giving the room the once over, he took his mobile out of his pocket. 'Hi, its me,' he said, when the call was picked up from the other end. 'The layout is exactly the same as the last monastery, right down to the finest detail.'

He listened for a moment, then with a sharp nod, said, 'OK.' Slipping his phone into his pocket, he slowly opened the door and looked up and down the corridor, checking that it was empty before slipping out and heading for his room.

In his bathroom, he stared into his mirror. To shave his beard off would be risky. Even though it had been a few years since he'd been a prisoner in France, the Leader might still recognize him. He ran his fingers through his thick black hair. Only one thing to do.

Picking his razor up, he started with his beard. Fifteen minutes later, he touched his bare scalp.

'Smooth as a baby's bum,' he muttered. 'It'll have to do, I can hardly recognize myself.'

A few minutes later he was back downstairs, taking his place by the window and gaining a nod of approval from the other guard.

LONDON

CHAPTER TWENTY-TWO

Smiler stared down at his plate. Rita had done him proud. There was everything you could wish for on a full English breakfast, except for the tomatoes. Smiler hated tomatoes. Only trouble was, even though it looked scrumptious, he felt sick to his stomach.

However, he would have to try his best to eat it, seeing as Rita had gone to so much trouble. Cutting into the pork sausage, he stabbed a piece with his fork and raised it slowly to his mouth, remembering the many times he'd raked through hotel dustbins just to find a piece of sausage like this.

He sighed heavily, and Rita, in full war paint, looked up from her own plate at him. Looking back at her, Smiler thought that was something else that was taking a bit of getting used to. Sometimes Rita was Robert, who said to call him Rob, and he'd only met Rob recently and somehow still kept calling him Robert, though he'd known Rita for a few years.

'What's wrong, chuck?'

Smiler shook his head. 'It's Mike. He's in a really bad way and I can't help him, it's as if he's shrouded. All I can see when I try is swirling clouds of grey...I can't even see his face any more.'

'No idea at all where he might be?'

Smiler shook his head. 'I've tried. I keep getting the feeling of metal scraping against metal, it's doing my head in. I think... well, I'm almost certain that he's a prisoner somewhere.'

'Me too.' Rita sighed. 'Although I'm pretty sure I know the region, something about the odd flash I'm getting, but I can't quite put my finger on it.'

'So what now?'

'Well, Aunt May arrived in Norwich a few hours ago, so I'm expecting a phone call shortly.'

Almost before Rita stopped speaking, the mobile rang. Grinning, she winked at Smiler and fished around in the pocket of her pink velour tracksuit. Smiler had nearly died when she walked in with it on, and just barley stopped short of asking if they'd been suddenly transported back to the eighties.

They had talked for a long time when they arrived back home last night. Smiler had eventually gone to bed in the early dawn, feeling slightly better in himself, and actually feeling quite sad for his mother - something he had thought he never would, in a million years. He had despised her for as long as he could remember, and the older he got, the worse he felt about her. But as Rita had explained to him, his mother had after all been as much a victim of the families as anyone had. Her whole life had been stolen by them, used and abused from an early age. If she hadn't managed to escape to protect her unborn baby from them, then God only knew where he himself would be now. The way she had died had been tragic. And over the years, there had been countless girls like his mother. His hands clenched into fists. They have to pay!

He gritted his teeth as he clenched his fists under the table. One way or another they fucking well will.

'OK, good news,' Rita said, as she closed her mobile and slipped it back into her pocket.

Smiler looked expectantly at her.

'You'll be pleased to hear that they think they have found out where Mike is.'

Smiler brightened right up. 'Where?'

Rita sighed and pulled a face. 'Well, he's only gone and got himself locked up in one of the families' biggest strongholds.'

'Ha! What do you expect? It's Mike Yorke we're talking about here, he does nothing by halves.' Smiler got his cigarettes out. 'So what now?' he asked, after lighting one up.

'Now we carry on with what we do best, Smiler. But first we have to meet someone.' Rita waved the cloud of smoke away. 'Please, Smiler, outside for the fags.'

'Sorry…Who?'

'What?' Rita was momentarily distracted.

'Who we gonna meet?'

'I'll tell you in a mo. He'll be here shortly anyhow. Then we'll set off in an hour or so, let the rush hour traffic get out of the way, should have eased off by then.'

'OK, but aren't you going to--'

'Get rid of the pink?' Rita laughed. 'Yes, right now, chuck.'

Smiler walked outside to finish his cigarette, wishing Mike was here now to do his usual borrowing act.

Gornal Library

www.better.org.uk/Gornal
Tel: 01384 812755

Borrowed Items : 24/06/2022 11:08
Customer ID: ********0630

Loaned today

Title: Before the storm
Due back: 22/07/2022

Title: unwanted guest
Due back: 22/07/2022

Title: Final countdown
Due back: 22/07/2022

Total item(s) loaned today: 3
Previous Amount Owed: 0.00 GBP
Overdue: 0
Reservation(s) pending: 0
Reservation(s) to collect: 0
Total item(s) on loan: 4

Items you already have on loan
Love your life
Due back: 06/07/2022

NORTHUMBERLAND

CHAPTER TWENTY-THREE

Sergeant Angela Rafferty put the phone down in her office and gave a self-satisfied smile. She had just been informed by the hospital that Detective Cox was fighting for his life, and had less than a twenty percent chance of pulling through. Even if he did, there was no guarantee that he would ever recover completely.

'Not good odds,' she muttered. 'For him, anyway.' Again she gave a small self-satisfied smile, knowing that the people she reported to would be happy.

Moving over to the small round mirror she'd recently hung on her office wall, and taking a bright red lipstick out of her handbag, she used it and smiled at her reflection. Turning sideways, she admired her navy slacks and red shirt. Picking up her navy cardigan, she slipped it over her shoulders, dropped the lipstick back into her handbag and snapped it shut.

Anyhow, that's him rid of, and he'll be easily finished off if nature doesn't do it. Why on earth didn't the idiot sent to do the job use a direct shot through the brain in the first place? She shook her head. Fool. He should have lost his hand, not just his stupid thumb.

Doubt if he'll be used by the families anymore.

She shrugged and muttered, 'He's probably at the bottom of the sea by now, sharing a deep watery grave with others of his kind. Cock up, and that's it. Unloved. Unwanted. Family law.'

A cock-up was the last thing Rafferty intended for herself. A distant cousin of Earl Simmonds on the Irish side of the family from Dublin, she knew she was a small cog in a big wheel and had to work hard to earn her keep. But she was family loyal, and would do anything, anything at all in their name.

Anyhow, she thought, that was Cox off her back regarding the Brodzinski brat. All she had to do now was find out where she and that Shelly Monroe bitch had flown to. Weird how they had both more or less dropped off the radar together. Rising, she went over to a steel filing cabinet, opened the top drawer and took a brown folder out. Removing a few sheets of paper, she quickly shredded them, all of the time looking over her shoulder in case someone walked in.

She finished destroying all trace of Annya Brodzinski. Not that anyone should even think of her, once I've dealt with her interfering nosy old grandfather. It will be as if the brat has never even existed. He's lived too long anyhow.

 She returned the empty folder to the cabinet and, picking up the phone, requested a driver to be out the front at once.

Five minutes later, blonde police driver Susan Cleverly pulled up outside the entrance door where Rafferty waited for her.

'Took your time, didn't you?' Rafferty snapped at her, then tutted as she brushed imaginary fluff off the car seat before climbing into the back of the car.

'Sorry, the water for the wipers needed topping up,' Constable Cleverly said, in her usual quiet unassuming manner.

'Take the road to Holy Island. But first, as it's on the way, call at Mr Brodzinski's. I have something to tell him.'

'Yes, Sergeant Rafferty.' She started the car and eased slowly into the morning traffic.

Behind her, Rafferty studied the constable's profile in the rear view mirror. Cleverly was a pretty young woman, with natural blonde hair and large blue eyes, and a tiny mole on her right cheek.

There's something about this one that needs watching, she thought. Never really noticed it before, but when I come to think about it, she always seems to be there when something's going on, sort of on the sidelines.

She narrowed her eyes. Going to have to check this one out. There's more than one driver in the pool, that's for sure. But whenever I ask for one, it's always her.

Too much of a coincidence!

Who's she really working for?

Reaching Mr Brodzinski's house, Cleverly pulled to a stop outside. Getting out of the car, Rafferty ordered her to stay where she was.

Cleverly glared at the other woman's back as she walked up the path to the old man's house, praying that he wasn't in. She had a feeling that Rafferty meant to kill him, and felt helpless. There was no way she could blow her cover.

Rafferty banged on the door. She waited a moment and banged again, so loudly that even anyone who was troubled with deafness would hear her. That included the woman next door, who opened her own door and glared at Rafferty.

'He's not in. And is there really need to bang on somebody's door like that?'

'You sure he's not in?'

'Yes, I'm sure. Who are you, like?'

Stupid question, Rafferty thought, seeing as there's a police car at the gate. Rafferty took her badge out, flashed it with a superior look on her face, and the woman shrugged.

'Whatever. He's still not in.' With a toss of her head, she slammed her front door.

Cleverly hid a smile as, obviously foaming with anger, Rafferty got back into the car. 'Holy Island,' she snapped.

They reached the causeway, which was clear of the sea apart from a few lingering puddles, and a few minutes later they were on the island. Rafferty told the driver to pull over into the car park and wait for her there.

Getting out of the car, she headed up towards the village, passing a fruit and veg stall with a smiling proprietor, whom she ignored with her usual disdain. She walked on past a large hotel, giving it the once over, and the same to a café on the corner, where a dozen or so tourists were eating.

Turning left into the main street, she went on down past a few cottages and the Lindisfarne Scriptorium shop. Carrying on past The Ship, she turned left into Sandham Lane and, pleased to get out of the way of the many tourists heading towards the castle, walked along the road to Aunt May's cottage.

She'd been surprised when the message had come through that she was to check out Mike Yorke's Aunt May's cottage, and to deal with a certain detective who may or may not be there. Having only met Mike's Aunt May the once, she'd had her down as nothing more than a nosy old crow of a woman, who she hadn't liked on sight. But her eyes had been bright and clear, and she remembered at the time thinking that this one was a lot sharper than people would ever give her credit for. It had felt at the time as if the woman had been looking right through her.

Although, on second thoughts, there's nothing to worry about. A nosy old crow's probably all she is, anyhow. But orders are orders, she thought, looking at the flower-covered cottage with a scowl.

I suppose, seeing as she likes the pathetic cow who calls herself a detective, that she's nosy enough to get involved. 'Well, God help the old bat!'

Back at the car park, Susan had her mobile phone out and was listening intently to whoever was speaking on the other end.

After a few minutes she closed her phone and looked towards the village. She's never been on Holy Island before, and wished she'd come with better company. Locking the car up, she followed the route taken by Rafferty.

CHAPTER TWENTY-FOUR

Although Kristina had been slightly panicked by the word "NOW", she'd been so exhausted that, when she sat back to think things through, and without meaning to, she'd somehow fallen asleep and slept right through the night.

Waking up, she stretched, yawned and glanced at the clock.

'Friggin' hell.' She gasped in shock. She'd slept ten hours straight.

'No way.'

Giving her head a shake, she hurried up to the bathroom. After using the toilet, she washed her hands then splashed cold water on her face before running back downstairs. Grabbing the letter up from the floor, she studied it for a minute again, only then noticing the picture of a fish scrawled on the bottom. Then it dawned on her just who Aunt May meant.

When she and Mike Yorke had been an item, they had gone sea fishing a few times with an old friend of Aunt May's. She and Mike had often wondered if the fisherman and Aunt May had once been more than just friends. Well, if she was honest, it had mostly been she who had done the wondering. Mike had been totally adamant that they were just good friends. Of course, in Mike's eyes, and Tony and Brother David's, Aunt May was a saint.

'And so she is,' Kristina muttered with a smile, as she quickly put her coat on and grabbed her bag.

She was just about to turn the handle on the front door when someone banged on the other side. Jumping in shock, she then froze for a moment, wondering what to do.

It could be anyone. The milkman?

Does Aunt May get her milk delivered?

Is there even a milkman on the island?

Or it could be someone else.

Someone she didn't want to see.

Who even knows I'm here?

The banging came again, galvanising her into action. Quietly, she ran upstairs to look out of the bedroom window. Gently easing the curtain along, she peered out. For a moment she was taken aback to see Sergeant Rafferty standing there, glowering at the door.

'Shit.'

What to do?

Like Brodzinski, Kristina didn't trust the woman either, and this call after what happened last night... How does she know I'm here? Should I let her in, or make a run for it?

The Island must have been cut off for most of the night, thank God, she thought, shuddering at the thought of how vulnerable she'd been. To run was her best, and probably only, option. Especially as Rafferty, as if she'd heard Kristina's thoughts, moved her head to look up at the bedroom window.

Kristina quickly dropped the curtain and leaned back against the wall, praying the woman hadn't seen the curtain twitch.

Time I was out of here.

Quietly she hurried down the stairs, through the sitting room and into the kitchen. She reached the back door and lifted her hand to the handle, hoping that someone had finally oiled the annoying squeak that had been there when she used to visit before.

Slowly she lifted the old latch. For a very brief second, there was a barely discernible scraping sound, then the latch lifted to its full and the door started to swing open.

Well, thank God for that! she thought.

NORWICH

CHAPTER TWENTY-FIVE

The door handle turned slowly, ever so slowly. Mike watched anxiously, a frown on his face, wondering if his tormentors had come to gloat, or to bring him another beating. Never before in his whole life had he felt so vulnerable.

It opened to reveal a dark-haired young woman who looked slightly familiar. I've seen her before, but where?

She closed the door behind her and crossed the large room in moments. Reaching his bed, she looked down at him, her eyes missing nothing. Then, with a sarcastic sneer, she said, 'Well, hello, brother.'

Brother! Mike gulped. No wonder I fucking well thought I knew her, I look at virtually the same face in the mirror every day. Lost for words, Mike could only stare at Lovilla.

He couldn't describe how he felt, how he had felt since he had woken up and found himself naked and chained to the bed, rehashing the night before. To go from orphan status to having a father, brother and now a sister overnight, when he'd always thought he was alone in the world, was a complete shock to his system, especially finding that said brother was nothing more than a callous, selfish bully.

How many more fucking relatives were going to come crawling out of the woodwork? he wondered.

He'd had dreams when he'd been a child, as any parentless kid had. That he was a lost prince who would one day claim the throne of England, had been only one of them. Grand dreams, but commonly shared by children who find out they are adopted. Then he'd grown up, and reality had kicked in. He had no blood ties with anyone. That was, until now.

It had been hard as a kid, especially when another kid had tried to bully him by shouting 'Bastard!' every time he passed in the school corridor. In the end he'd fairly lost it, and the kid had ended up in hospital. The shame of it was, the kid had been the same age as he, nine, and must have heard his stupid parents talking without taking care that small ears were listening. But with the help of Aunt May, Tony and Dave, he had made it. He knew that without them he would have been nothing.

He looked this new sister up and down, pretty much the same way she had looked at him.

'Sister, eh...' Mike shook the hand that was tied to the bed. The handcuffs rattled. 'OK. Gonna do the sisterly thing, then, and get me outta this mess?'

Lovilla laughed. 'I doubt it. Me, help an outbreed?' She looked down her nose at him with unconcealed contempt. 'As if!'

Mike frowned. 'What do you mean, an outbreed?'

She tutted, then as if explaining the sex life of bees to a small child, she carried on. 'An outbreed, or an illegal, is either a son or daughter born to one of the families out of wedlock and to a common peasant. You' - she emphasised the 'You' with a curl of her top lip - 'are one of thousands. Nothing more than an ugly subhuman, really. Probably stupid as well.'

Well, that's me put in my place, he thought, but said, 'Yeah, well, the jury's out on that one, sis. So, you have a name? Or do I just call you "your Highness"?'

She glared at him for a moment, then snapped, 'What? How dare you use sarcasm on me!'

'It wasn't hard.'

Stepping closer, she laid her hand flat on his chest. 'Have you any idea at all just who you're dealing with, peasant?'

'No, but I just bet you're gonna tell me.'

Angrily, her fingers closed and she grabbed a handful of his black chest hair. She twisted hard, then quickly yanked it out.

It hurt, and Mike winced but, gritting his teeth, he refused to give her the satisfaction that it actually more than hurt. His chest was on fire, and he felt like screaming. Instead, he smiled at her.

Even more angry that she had not got the reaction she wanted, she jumped away from him and snapped, 'Peasant bastard.' Then, turning away, she stormed towards the door.

'Some sister,' Mike called after her, thinking she had been just short of stamping her feet like a small child.

Turning back, she snarled, 'I am no sister to a filthy outbreed. I don't know who the fucking hell you think you are, but news flash…you are nothing. And God knows what they are planning for you, but expect no help from me. Or my brother.'

'Him, I've already met.'

'Then you'll know what he'll do without me having to tell you.' She laughed, tossed her head and slammed the door behind her.

Guess I know exactlywhere I stand with her, then, Mike thought ruefully.

He stared at the ceiling for a moment, wondering again how the hell he was going to get out of this.

LONDON

CHAPTER TWENTY-SIX

Danny stepped down from the plane. The flight had been smooth and quiet, as the man who had pulled him into the car at Berwick, and practically pulled him out of the car again at Newcastle airport, had barely spoken a single word the whole time - even though Danny had done his best to question him.

He was a youngish man with fair hair, and a face that only a mother could love. His dark blue suit looked at least two sizes too big for him, as if he'd recently lost a fair bit of weight or borrowed it from an overweight friend. And he had totally failed to reassure Danny that he was not one of them, replying to his questions time and time again with nothing more than a series of grunts.

Sure, Danny was thinking as they slowly made their way through customs, he hasn't said that he is one of them, but he hasn't really said that he's not one of them either.

Which leaves me where?

Out on a fucking limb as usual.

Snatching his passport back, he received a suspicious look from the woman customs officer, plus a sniff, accompanied by a glare from the male officer next to her, when she used her elbow to nudge him as she whispered something.

Danny shrugged and pulled a couldn't-care-less face. He could still smell the wet dog himself, and so had quite a few people on the plane, judging by the looks they had thrown his way.

'So really bothered like…Not!' he muttered, scowling every which way as he followed the man through the airport doors.

Should I make a run for it? Danny was thinking now as they headed over towards the car park. He looked around him. Should be easy. The silent freak doesn't look all that fit, and I'll sharp get lost amongst all these people. Bet there's been a thousand come through here today, anyone of them could belong to the fucking families.

A breeze blew up from nowhere, and he got a strong whiff of his clothes.Jesus he thought, pulling a face.With a sigh his thoughts went back to the predicament he was in.

Yeah, but where would I run to?

'Cos for a fucking fact, all they would need was one sniffer dog with half a fucking nose.

What the hell do I know about London? Only been here the once, for fuck's sake.

And it rained the whole friggin' time!

'Get in,' the man said suddenly. They had weaved their way through at least a hundred cars, Danny banging his elbows on the wing mirrors of most of them, before they finally reached a dirty white Mini.

'You could've parked it a bit closer,' Danny grumbled, only to be ignored. 'And gave it a wash.' Receiving a glowering look, Danny shrugged.

'Where we going, like?'

This got an answer of sorts. 'To see Shelly.'

'Wow, was that a sentence you just uttered?' Danny exaggeratedly wiped his brow. 'Please, hold me up.'

Ignoring Danny's attempts to draw him into conversation, the man went to put his hand on Danny's head. Danny brushed it off and got into the car himself, thinking, Copper! Only a copper would do that. 'Cos that's what they're fucking well trained to do when putting people they've arrested into cars. Seen it on the telly loads of times.

Not sure if the thought that the quiet man might be a copper pleased him or not. Plenty bent coppers around, seen that on the telly an' all. And heard about it from a mate or two.

Danny fastened the seat belt, and watched as the man walked around the car and got in.

He shot a smile at Danny, which really freaked him out, and set him off babbling. 'Look, why don't you just tell me where Shelly is, eh, and I'll go find her myself. It'll be much easier for you instead of trailing around in all this traffic… Just give me the address, mate, no need to bother yourself any longer.'

'No.'

'Why not? You can just jog off home. Put your feet up, 'cos you look really tired. OK, so just tell me where she is and point me in the right direction.' Nodding his head, Danny loosened the seatbelt.

'Fasten it,' the man growled at him.

'Screw you.'

Another growl, accompanied by a glare. 'OK, OK.' Danny hastily refastened the belt. 'OK, OK, keep your hair on. Just an idea, that's all, mate. No need to get all het up about it. For fuck's sake.'

Feeling totally helpless, he sighed and stared out of the car window as they left the car park and pulled into the traffic, wondering if he dare jump out of the car if they came to a stop somewhere.

A moment later, that plan was cast aside as he heard the central locking system click on.

He was a prisoner again.

CHAPTER TWENTY-SEVEN

Tony Driver stood outside the door of the small pet shop in one of Soho's narrow back streets, idly watching the crowds passing by. He remembered reading somewhere that Soho had once been a hunting ground, and legend had it that it got its name from hunters crying out, 'So ho!' as they rode through the fields after their prey. Damn hard to imagine this busy place as once being rolling green fields.

Back then it had actually been built up as a destination for the rich, but they soon disappeared when Soho was hit by a cholera outbreak in 1854. He guessed that most of the families would have had a stake in the land, as they still owned most of the property, pubs, and brothels around here. They probably started the cholera outbreak on purpose. And there had always, since biblical times, been a hell of a lot of profit in prostitution.

He sighed. Times change, he thought, but the families have always been constant. But not any more. And what better place to hide, than out in the open!

He looked in the window. Mike would love this shop, full of fluffy puppies and kittens, plus some quite exotic animals. A small striped snake in the window suddenly raised its head and hissed at him, and Tony involuntarily stepped back, even though there was a glass window between them.

He smiled at his reflection in the window and straightened his blue tie, his thoughts skipping from the snake back to Mike Yorke. Mike had bought this tie for his birthday last year.

Why the fuck didn't you just lie low, Mike?

He glanced at his gold watch, a very expensive present from one of the Egyptians. Bribery indeed, but something he would be a fool to decline. If any of them thought he had any morals at all, it would be his death warrant.

Moving towards the door of the shop, he entered and nodded his head at grey-haired bespectacled Muriel behind the counter, who was much more than the sign on the shop window would have you believe. She smiled at him as he opened a metal door on the right-hand side of the counter.

The room he entered was windowless, and obviously an office of some sort. A large square conference table stood in the middle of the floor, with a coffee urn and half a dozen mugs. On the side facing him sat three men. Whatever they had been discussing before he came in, silence reigned now.

Tony took his place at the table, facing them, and was greeted by smiles and hellos from the three men.

Dr Raymond Vickers, a small black man with greying hair, and small round gold-rimmed spectacles, was a specialist in childhood disease. He asked, in a South African accent, 'So, just about every-thing in place then?' He smiled, one of pleased relief. There was an air of excitement about him as if something he'd wanted for a long time was about to happen.

Tony nodded, as the other two men leaned closer over the table. 'I think this is the real start of it. We have a lot of people in place now. Soon, hopefully in the next few years, none but a very few of the fam-ilies will remain.'

All three sat back with satisfied smiles on their faces.

'At last,' Derek Quinn, the American vice president said. 'It's been a long time coming.' He fiddled with the right side of his brown moustache, as he looked at the other two.

'And the transmission, it will be smooth?' asked Lars Abendroth, a German priest, a small, very portly man with only one arm, who had always refused to wear a prosthetic limb.

Unable to completely share their optimism, Tony looked at all three of them in turn. These were the headmen, along with a very courageous woman who had carried the fight their ancestors had started into this century. Only a fool would think that the families did-n't know about them. They knew all right, but they didn't know just how organised the rebellion was. Finally, when the priest was starting to show some agitation, he said, 'As smooth as it can possibly be. Of course, there will always be rumours, waves, speculations, but the truth of what will happen, and what has happened in the past, will be kept hidden, hopefully forever.'

'And the keeper of the book? She is well?'

Tony smiled. 'Very well.'

The vice president said, 'Well, this will be our last meeting, this side of' - he shrugged - 'the surprise.'

The others nodded, as Tony was thinking, 'Sad that they are so naive. A thousand things can go wrong. So easily.'

NORTHUMBERLAND

CHAPTER TWENTY-EIGHT

In less time than it takes to draw breath, Kristina reached the back gate. Quickly pulling the bolt out, she was halfway through before it was even properly open. The sea was in front of her, and to the right, about a half a mile away, was the fisherman's cottage. A dozen or so upended boats surrounded the blue-washed cottage. The ground was uneven, but Kristina was pretty fit and guessed she could run the distance in a few minutes. That was before, she was suddenly grabbed by the throat.

'Going somewhere?' Rafferty asked, her grip tightening as she pinned Kristina against the wall.

Kristina quickly reacted by bashing her on the side of her head with her bag and, at the same time, jumping on Rafferty's toes.

The woman grinned at her, but Kristina, yelling like a banshee, then grabbed a handful of Rafferty's hair, yanking her head to the side. Rafferty screamed and let go of Kristina's throat, but lashed out at her face with her nails, drawing blood from two deep scratches. Kristina pushed her hard enough for Rafferty to fall over, then without hesitation took off in the direction of the cottage.

By the time Rafferty scrambled to her feet, Kristina was out of sight. Guessing the direction she'd headed, Rafferty ran in a beeline for the blue-washed cottage.

It was only a few minutes before she spotted Kristina. The sight of her spurred Rafferty on, and she began swiftly, step by step, to close in on her. 'Got you now, you bitch,' she muttered, as each second brought her closer to her prey.

For a brief moment, Kristina disappeared as she ran down a small dip in the ground. Then she appeared at the top, looking behind her at Rafferty, who was now close enough to see the fear in her eyes, and grinned at her.

A moment later, Rafferty was pushed from behind, and she went spinning down the bank.

LONDON

CHAPTER TWENTY-NINE

Sitting in the chair by the fireplace, staring out of the window, but seeing nothing of the sunshine, nor the buses, cars and people passing by, Smiler flicked the ash off his cigarette, completely missing the ash tray. The ash landed on Tiny's back who, feeling nothing through his thick coat of hair, slumbered on at Smiler's feet.

Smiler was trying as hard as he could to see Mike, but it was so hopeless. He knew, without knowing how, that somehow he was being blocked by someone or something. Frustratingly, where Mike should be in his mind, there were nothing but numbers again. And once more he had no idea what they meant. All he could think that it meant was a silent count down to nowhere.

He looked down and saw not one but three or four strands of ash on the dog's back. 'Shit...sorry, mate.' Smiler rubbed the ash off Tiny's back.

All-forgiving, as was his dog way, Tiny rose to his full height and, standing on his back legs, placed his front paws on Smiler's chest, giving him a huge slavery kiss.

Grimacing, Smiler wiped his face then put his arms around the big dog and hugged him. A moment later, he looked into the dog's deep brown eyes and said, 'Jesus, mate. Don't want to hurt your feelings, like, but your breath so stinks.'

Tiny wagged his tail.

'Come on, mate, we've got plenty of time. We'll head down to the pet shop, get something to clean your teeth, scruffy mutt.'

Still wagging his tail, Tiny got down and stood still while Smiler snapped his lead on.

'And where do you think you two are off to?' Rita asked, coming up the hallway behind them. 'Don't forget, we're off in an hour or so.' Rita looked at her watch. 'The person we're waiting for should be here shortly, that's if the traffic's been OK.'

'We won't be long,' Smiler said, opening the door. 'Just off to the pet shop. Give you time to put your slap on.'

Rita tossed her head, and went back upstairs.

Near the end of the long street of terraced houses, Smiler frowned. Was it suddenly getting darker? He looked up at the sky with a puzzled look on his face.

No rain clouds around.

A few more steps, and Tiny whined low in his throat. Smiler's uneasiness increased. 'What's the matter, boy?'

Tiny whined again, and sat down. A moment later, he stood and turned in the direction of home. It was then that Smiler heard a voice he knew.

'You owe me.'

Whispered in a menacing tone in his ear, as if the person was standing next to him.

'No.' Smiler said out loud, looking quickly around, expecting to see Snakes at any minute.

'What... Where?' Smiler muttered, when there was no one in sight.

Tiny whined even louder, and started pulling on his lead. Pulling Smiler towards home and safety.

But Smiler was rooted to the spot in fear. Tiny started to bark. He kept looking at Smiler, then turning to look homewards. Finally he moved quickly up to Smiler and started nudging him, each nudge punctuated with a swift bark.

But it wasn't until a car pulled up alongside them that Smiler blinked and stared at the driver.

What the fuck's he doing? Danny thought. Could he have found a rougher looking fucker than him to ask directions from?

But instead of asking directions from the youth with the smile carved on his face, the driver jumped out of the car and bundled the youth into the front seat. Grabbing the dogs lead, he ushered him into the back next to Danny,

'What the fuck?' Danny yelled, pushing at the dog who, his tail wagging like crazy, seemed intent on swallowing him whole, out of the way.

'What the fucking hell?' Smiler said scowling at Danny.

'Shut up both of you,' the driver said, as he took off along the street, stopping outside of the house Smiler had just left a few minutes ago.

Danny was still trying to brush off Tiny's friendly intentions when the driver opened the door to let them out.

'Must be more good in you than I thought,' the driver said to Danny, who blinked his puzzlement at the longest speech he'd heard from the man in all of their travels.

The man nodded his head towards Tiny. 'The dog! He knows.'

Danny looked down at Tiny. He raised his hand, unsure whether to pat the huge beast or not, the risk of losing his hand uppermost in his mind, even though the dog seemed friendly enough. Actually over-friendly, Danny thought, scowling at Tiny. As if I don't stink of friggin' dog enough. Then the man said, 'Quickly, inside.'

The urgency in the man's voice was infectious. Smiler, Danny, and even the dog scuttled quickly in through the gate and down the path into the house.

Coming through into the kitchen from the opposite direction, at the same time as they all tumbled in through the door, Rita stared at them for a moment, before nodding her head. 'It's the electricity charge in the air, Smiler. A build-up, that's all, their far-seers trying to find you.'

'Guess they nearly did.' Smiler shivered.

'Didn't the dog warn you?'

Smiler looked down at Tiny. 'I guess he tried to.'

'Take notice of him in future, Smiler. Dogs are very sensitive to this sort of stuff.'

'What fucking sort of stuff?' Danny demanded, sick of being handed to one stranger after another like an unwanted parcel. Then he went on impatiently, 'You want to know something?' He looked Rita up and down. 'It doesn't matter. I'm just about fucked off with everything.' He turned to go, only to find his way out blocked by his travelling companion.

'And you can fuck off an' all, Mr fucking Happy.'

'Danny, calm down,' Rita said softly.

Danny spun back round. Shaking his head, he stared at Rita. She was dressed in a yellow sundress with matching high heels, and her blonde wig curled on her shoulders. 'You know what? I don't care any more. Do you know what I think, eh? Do you?'

Rita nodded.

'I think I've been right all along. I'm locked up in some nut house, and all this is nowt but a fucking dream. 'Cos you wanna know what, Mr…Mrs…whatever…you are just about the final fucking straw.'

Smiler quickly moved in front of Rita and faced Danny. 'Watch your fucking mouth when you're talking to her.'

'Or what?' Danny squared up to Smiler. Never the bravest of souls, Danny had finally reached the end. This lot and their fucking dog could just fuck off. He raised his fists to Smiler.

Quickly Rita inserted herself between them. 'OK, that's enough, we're all on the same side. Now, come on. Let's go sit down and talk this through.'

'Best of luck,' the man said, giving Rita a wave as he walked out the door.

'And who the fuck's he? The bastard hasn't said more than half a dozen fucking words the whole time I've been with him.'

'Come on, I'll explain.'

'Explain!' Danny said, under his breath. 'This I gotta hear.'

'Shut up, fuck face,' Smiler snapped.

Danny glared at Smiler. 'You gotta be kidding.'

'Enough.' Rita pushed Smiler in the direction of the sitting room.

Without looking at each other, Smiler led the way and Danny followed Rita into the sitting room, with Tiny bringing up the rear.

Sitting down in the brown leather chair beside the fire that Rita offered him, Danny muttered, 'This better be good.'

Rita and Smiler sat opposite him on the matching settee. Between them, an oak coffee table held half a dozen women's magazines. In the corner near the window there was a revolving globe on a metal stand, and a large pink orchid in full bloom in the window.

Seeing Danny looking at the magazines, Smiler said hastily, 'They aren't just for Rita. There's a few girls here as well.'

'Never said nowt.' Danny shrugged.

'No, but you--'

'All right, enough. Danny meet Smiler… Smiler meet Danny… Both of you have suffered greatly at the hands of the families, so please, I really need you to get along.'

'Why?' Danny asked.

'Yeah, why?' Smiler looked Danny up and down, then sniffed.

Danny narrowed his eyes at him.

Rita puffed the air out of her lungs, disturbing her heavy blonde fringe, as Danny and Smiler shrugged together in a move which looked as if it had been set by a choreographer.

NORWICH

CHAPTER THIRTY

Shelly dressed carefully, from the clothes in her wardrobe that Coral had filled the day before. She chose nondescript colours, matching various shades of grey, in leggings, long plain tunic top and short jacket, even managing to find a pair of grey shoes amongst the half-dozen pairs at the bottom of the wardrobe.

She had never bothered to ask where the clothes had come from, just accepted them as part of the service. What Coral, Ella and others around the country were doing was definitely a service, and a very noble one, too.

Looking in the mirror she decided against make up of any kind, and brushed her short, recently bleached blonde hair behind her ears.

She gave herself the once over and, satisfied that even her own brothers would never recognise her, slipped three fully loaded insulin pens into her pocket.

'Now to get out of here without anyone seeing me,' she said to the mirror, and headed for the door.

Slowly she opened it and, straining her ears and satisfied that there was no one in the immediate location, crept slowly along the hallway. Pausing a moment when she heard a low moaning coming from one of the bedrooms as she passed, she grimaced and thought, I know exactly what you're going through, love.

Reaching the back door into the garden, she slipped outside, past the pond, and was at the gate in seconds. Next minute, she was out in the street and closing the gate behind her.

It had been easy slipping Aunt May's purse out of her bag, when she went with Coral and Ella to check up on Annya. Lifting a twenty and ignoring the fifty, knowing it would bring strange looks when she tried to cash it in, she'd dropped the purse beside the chair, trying to make it look like it had fallen out of the bag.

Walking to the end of the street, she justified her theft, thinking that she would pay Aunt May back as soon as she could, and that, in the long run, they would thank her for what she was about to do. It was the only option she had. They certainly wouldn't let her go willingly, and that was a fact.

And this is something I have to do!

Even supposing it kills me, and it probably will. After all, no one really cares if I live or die.

Danny hates me. Annya hates me. Probably the whole fucking world hates me.

Five minutes later, she was in a taxi and heading for town. She knew just the bars she wanted, the routine that was used, and what worked before would surely work again. It would be easier and less suspicious if she was actually picked up from town.

An hour later, she was dancing in one of the town centre's busiest bars. She'd joined a girl who was way gone, and wouldn't know her own mother from a mad gorilla. Already she was behaving as if Shelly was her best friend.

'So,' Shelly said five minutes later, as she was propping her up in the queue for the Ladies. 'Where did you get the gear from, then?'

The girl, small and elfin-featured with long black hair, giggled, put her hand over her mouth and muttered, 'Not supposed to say till they've seen you.'

'You can tell me, though, can't you, Sarah? We're best friends, aren't we?'

For a moment, the girl looked at her as if she didn't have a clue who she was. Then, grinning, she muttered, 'Course I can. You're my best friend, ain't you... See him over there?' She motioned with her head towards a young guy standing at the bar.

Shelly looked over to her right. It was hard to pick faces out in the dimly-lit club. 'No,' the girl nudged her, 'over that way. Him leaning against the bar, with the red shirt on... Ooh, if we don't hurry up, I'm gonna pee right here on the floor!'

'Won't be long. Look, we're moving again.'

'Good, 'cos--'

But Shelly wasn't listening. She had already disappeared as, frowning, the girl looked around for her.

Shelly circled the room and stood a few yards away from the young man, looking him up and down. Dark-haired and clean-shaven, he looked fresh out of college at first glance, not the druggie type. But as Shelly knew well, you couldn't always tell. Some showed their addictions a lot more than others. Though in the end, they all paid the price.

She knew that the Leader liked the men and boys clean-shaven, just the same as he liked the girls to have long black hair. Guess this is it, then, she thought, moving closer. My ticket in!

He turned then, and caught Shelly looking at him. On cue, she smiled and moved next to him.

Pretending to be drunk, she put her arm over his shoulder and whispered in his ear.

'What makes you think I'll have anything like that on me?' he said, a touch of mock anger in his voice. 'Somebody said something, have they?' He looked around.

Shelly shrugged. 'No, just thought you might... you know, know somebody?'

He studied her for a moment, then smiled. 'You tried the new stuff yet, babes?'

'No, but I've heard it's mind-blowing, all right. Why? You got some on you?' She batted her eyelids at him.

He slipped his arm around her waist. 'Come with me.'

Arm in arm, they went outside to the car park. 'Fancy a drive?'

'Where to?'

'Well, got no stuff on me now. Actually,' he grinned, as he ran his forefinger down the middle of her cleavage, 'sold out today much quicker than anticipated.'

'OK.' She smiled at him, even though what she really wanted was to snap his finger off and shove it right up his arse. ' Why not?'

'Come on, then.' He took her hand and led her over to his car, a white open-topped sports type. He opened the door for her, then went round to his side. Jumping in, he started the engine. As they drove out of the car park, he asked her name.

'Sss...Sandy. What's yours?'

He didn't answer. Instead he winked at her.

'So, where are we going, babes?'

He stared at her for a moment before smiling. 'To a place you are just going to love.'

I just bet I am, she thought, smiling back at him.

CHAPTER THIRTY-ONE

Staring out of the bedroom window, Tarasov turned and glared at the slave girl as she placed his clothes on the bed. This one had puzzled him for a while, she reminded him of someone from way back.

'Where do you originate from, peasant?' he suddenly snapped.

Startled, she dropped his shirt on the floor.

'Clumsy. Re-press it.'

'Yes, sir.' Quickly, she picked the shirt up and hurried into the small utility room.

'Come back.'

She appeared in the doorway a second later, shirt still in hand, a terrified look on her face.

'You have not answered my question.'

She swallowed hard. 'From, from Newcastle, sir.'

'Newcastle?' He had memories of Newcastle. 'Newcastle in the northeast of England?'

'Yes, sir.'

'Did you know the girl who escaped?'

'Not really, sir.'

Tarasov stared at her, but he wasn't really listening. His mind had wandered off to a woman he had once loved. The only woman he had ever loved. Not his wife, Juliana - that had only been a marriage of convenience, with one of the families. She had given birth to his two legal children, then conveniently died.

No, this woman had somehow found her way into his heart as no other person ever had. Then, shortly after giving birth to the out-breed Mike Yorke, she had disappeared. No matter how hard he'd tried, with every resource on earth, he had never found her. Could this girl somehow be related to her?

She comes from the same city.

'Your parents, you know both?'

She nodded.

'Speak, girl. Tell me about them.'

His heart had dipped for a moment when she'd indicated that she had both parents, but that meant absolutely nothing. She could have been adopted.

'Are they your real parents?'

She nodded again.

'Speak, girl, or I'll have you beaten.'

Quickly she replied, 'They are both still alive.'

'And living where?'

'New…Newcastle.' She stared wide-eyed at him. 'Please don't hurt them.'

'Are you adopted?'

She shook her head.

'Is that no, you're not, or no, you don't know?'

'I'm not...Please don't hurt them.'

'I have no intentions of doing so.' He waved his hand at her. 'Get on with your work.'

He filled a glass with brandy, and sat down on a brown leather chair facing a huge TV screen. It was early, even by his standards, for alcohol, but he didn't intend on socialising where he would have to keep his wits about him. His intentions were to dwell on the past and a certain woman, and how she had managed to remain hidden from him for all these years.

It had been hot that day, all those years ago, a day much like today, when she'd disappeared into thin air on a trip to the north of England. He had not known she'd been pregnant at the time. It wasn't until the child had been in his twenties that, through a regular blood test that one of the family doctors had been carrying out, Mike Yorke had come to his notice.

But she had been the one who had changed him, the one person that had made him see that the way of the families was wrong. It had been easy to keep the pretence up, though once or twice he had nearly slipped up and had received a few strange looks from family members. It had only been recently that he'd been able to get his point across that the way was wrong.

He had instigated the change, and knew a few others thought the same as him. Definitely others down the centuries had thought the same, also. Ten years ago, the inner wheel of agents had been formed. So far they had managed to foil a few assassinations, which would have led to a lot more wars going on around the world. Plus his money, and that of a few others, were keeping solvent the safe houses scattered around the world.

He sipped from his glass, taking a moment to savour the fine old brandy. The wretched girl had certainly reminded him of Melissa. Same beautiful eyes, same face structure - though Melissa had never been cowed. Melissa had an air about her that screamed, 'Enjoy me while you can, 'cos I'm not stopping long.'

He smiled. She hadn't stopped long either, one beautiful summer and she had escaped.

CHAPTER THIRTY-TWO

Mike narrowed his eyes as the bedroom door opened and a small fair-haired woman, he guessed somewhere in her early twenties, slipped in.

Not another relative, he thought.

Ella quickly reached his bedside. 'Mike Yorke?'

'Yes, that's me. But I'm afraid you have me at a disadvantage.'

Ella looked him over and grinning, said, 'Yeah, rather.'

Putting the clothes she carried onto the bottom of the bed, she grabbed the key off the bedside table and set about loosening the handcuffs.

A few minutes later, Mike was fully dressed in a waiter's uniform. He flexed his arms. The black jacket was slightly tight across his shoulders and arms, but it did the job.

Ella nodded her head in satisfaction. 'You'll pass.'

'I better had. So what's the plan, and who are you working for?'

'Aunt May.'

'What?' Mike reeled with the news. 'You mean, my--'

'Yes.'

She stared at him as he digested what she'd said. She could see it was a problem, but one he would have to contemplate later. Time was of the essence. If they had any chance of escape without her being compromised, it had to be now.

'Come on, we've got to move. Remember, if we bump into any-one, anyone at all, keep your head down. Do not, unless it's demand-ed, look at their face... And you are not with me. I do not know you.' She expressed her words with feeling, and cut short what she was about to say - that for the greater good of all, everyone was expend-able, even Mike Yorke.

Mike nodded. 'OK, I get it.'

He followed her to the door. Slowly Ella opened it and looked up and down the corridor. Slipping quickly outside, she left Mike to close the door behind them, and hurried along to the lift. Close behind her, Mike's mind was racing, putting two and two together, only they added up to nothing.

'Damn! What the fucking hell is it that I don't know?' he mut-tered.

Reaching the lift without mishap, Ella frowned at him as she pressed the basement button. 'Remember, if there's anybody about, in the lift or downstairs, we don't know each other.'

'So what do I say if anyone asks?'

'You're new here OK. Better still, can you speak any foreign lan-guages?'

'A smattering of German, really just a few basic words.'

'That'll do. Not many Germans here, but perhaps a couple who are fluent, so pray we don't bump into them.'

The lift arrived. Both of them held their breath as the doors slowly opened, Ella nearly collapsing with relief when it was empty. Inside, she pressed the button for the basement.

'You could live in here,' Mike said, looking around the luxurious lift. 'What the hell's the rest of the place like, if the lift is as good as this?'

'Way more than luxurious,' Ella replied. The next moment, the lift slowed down and came to a stop on floor three.

'Shit,' she muttered, her heartbeat doubling as the doors started to open.

NORTHUMBERLAND

CHAPTER THIRTY-THREE

Susan Cleverly ran down the small incline, and reached the bottom at the same time as Rafferty stopped rolling. Grabbing her top with both hands, she hauled the shaken woman to her feet.

Rafferty tried to fight her off. Slapping Susan's face with her right hand, she reached for her hair with her left. But Susan, trained in more than one martial art, was too quick for her. Slipping her right foot behind Rafferty's right leg, she pushed hard against both of her shoulders, sending Rafferty back down to the ground. Rolling away from her, Rafferty jumped up and faced Susan.

'Back off, now! You don't know who you're dealing with. I mean it. One phone call, that's all it will take.'

Susan laughed in her face. 'Oh, I know only too well who I'm dealing with here. It's you who hasn't got a clue.' She stepped forward, her hands raised, just as Rafferty was about to run at her. Susan leapt forward, grabbed Rafferty's neck and twisted hard.

The strength needed to break someone's neck is much more than the average person has, even one trained in martial arts. As a slowing down tactic it worked well, though, giving Susan time to pull a knife from her pocket. She thrust upwards, stabbing Rafferty under her ribcage and into her heart. Twisting the blade, her face at first close to Rafferty's, Susan made eye contact, and watched the life disappear from Rafferty's eyes as she slowly slid to the ground.

'Now you know,' she muttered.

Stepping quickly back, she looked around. There was no one in sight. Taking a moment to wipe the blood off her knife and her hands on the grass, she then put the knife away, and quickly headed off in the direction taken by Kristina. In less than a minute, she was outside the blue-washed cottage.

The door was pulled open before she had a chance to knock. The man who stood there, fisherman Patrick Logan, smiled at her through his heavy black beard. Although in his late fifties, Patrick also had a full head of black hair. He stepped back, ushering her through, rummaging in his brown corduroy trousers for his pipe as he did so.

'Where did you come from?' Kristina asked, slightly amazed by Susan's appearance when she had been expecting Rafferty. She was still getting over the fact that Patrick had been expecting her and had welcomed her into his cottage with open arms, offering her a cup of tea, telling her in the same breath that they would be sailing in less than an hour with the tide. There would be no time, and it would be far too dangerous, to take her back home to pick up some of her belongings. With the tea, Patrick had brought a bowl of water and clean cloths for Katrina to wash the blood off her face, which is what she had been doing when Cleverly entered the cottage.

'There's a clean-up job for you back there, Patrick, two minutes walk in one of the dips to the right,' Susan said, indicating with her head the direction in which she'd left Rafferty.

Patrick nodded, knocking the spent tobacco out of his pipe in preparation of a new batch. 'I expected as much.' He looked at Kristina, with raised eyebrows. 'I won't be long.'

'Care to tell me just what the hell is going on?' Kristina asked, looking at Susan, when Patrick had closed the door behind him.

'Guess I'm gonna have to leave that to Aunt May. Really got to get back and cover my tracks, though I doubt anyone at the station is ever going to miss Sergeant Rafferty.'

Kristina frowned. 'Why, what have you done to her?'

'My job.'

Inside Kristina shivered. Constable Cleverly was no more the mild-mannered constable she'd thought she was. Just what the hell have I been missing?

'So what exactly is that?'

'Mainly to look after you, whatever it takes.'

Kristina raised her eyebrows. 'On whose orders?'

'Aunt May's.'

Kristina mulled it over for a minute, then asked, 'Just where does Aunt May fit into all of this?'

'Everywhere.'

'OK...'

'Look, just be patient. It's a long story. Aunt May will put you right when you get there.'

'Where?'

'Norwich.'

'OK, so--'

'Please. Here's Patrick… Come on, move it. Sorted?' Susan asked, as Patrick appeared in the doorway.

'Yes, just need a few things and we're off.'

A minute later, two of them were heading for Patrick's boat, while the third headed back to her car.

LONDON

CHAPTER THIRTY-FOUR

After filling the car up, receiving countless stares and ignoring them all, Rita strutted in her best pink high heels past the cars that were pulling up for petrol in the garage. She'd dumped the yellow sundress and settled for white jeans and a pink top, with huge pink and white hoop earrings.

The plan was to stock up on sandwiches, pop and crisps to save them stopping for dinner on the two-and-a-half hour journey to Norwich, which in reality, with the traffic, would probably be three hours. She winked at a big hairy white-van driver filling up at the last pump. She knew he was about to whistle, until he realised what she was and nearly had a heart attack. Grinning to herself, she went inside, picked a basket up and started filling it with the requested goodies for Danny and Smiler, not forgetting dog chews for Tiny.

She paid at the till with one of her many credit cards, marvelling to herself how she remembered each card number. The next time she needed one in London it would be a different card, so that she couldn't be traced from one place to the other.

Back in the car, Danny gently pushed Tiny's head away from his face as the dog seemed to be determined to lick him to death.

'Don't hurt him,' Smiler snapped, scowling at Danny.

'I'm not,' Danny snapped back. 'Wouldn't anyhow. What the fuck makes you think I would hurt any dog? I'm not a fucking monster, you know.'

'How do I know that, eh? Don't fucking know who you are. Could be a fucking paedo for all I know.'

Danny, his face red with anger, was about to retort when Rita came back. Handing a carrier bag over to Danny, she said, 'Come on now, girls, play nice please. And you sit down, Tiny. Now.'

Tiny immediately sat down and, tongue lolling out, tail whipping up a mini tornado, looked hopefully at Rita. Rita had deliberately seated Smiler and Danny together in the back of the car, hoping that they would get to know each other, and at least form a truce of sorts. She guessed that so far it wasn't working, judging by the looks they kept throwing at each other, along with the insults they kept trading when they did speak.

'Tell shit for brains I ain't no fucking paedo, will you? Before I just get up and fucking go,' Danny shouted at Rita.

'Smiler!' Rita said, glaring at him. 'What's got into you? Danny's nothing of the sort.'

Smiler tutted and looked the other way, while Danny pulled a face as he rummaged through the bag, pulling out a packet of salt and vinegar crisps, a Mars bar and a can of Diet Coke before handing the bag over to Smiler. Taking the bag Smiler, watched by Tiny, opened the dog chews first.

Most of the journey was spent in silence. No matter how many times Rita tried to start a conversation, on whatever subject, neither Danny nor Smiler were in the mood for small talk. Both of them sat staring out of the windows, a stubborn look on both their faces.

Giving up, Rita put on a CD of the Eagles' Greatest Hits and, turning the volume up high, thought, 'Like it or lump it, guys'.

About half an hour from Norwich, Rita pulled into another garage. Jumping out of the car, she went round to the boot and took a dark blue holdall out.

Danny heaved an impatient sigh, and gave a couldn't-care-less, one-shouldered shrug as Rita said, 'Won't be a minute, guys.'

'Tiny needs more water, Rita,' Smiler shouted after her.

'I'm on it,' she shouted back over her shoulder.

Ten minutes later, when she still wasn't back, Danny said, 'So where the hell is she...he?'

'She. When it's Rita, it's she, and when it's Robert, it's...'

That was as far as he got. A tall, dark-haired young man in black jeans and t-shirt strode out of the garage, up to the car and opened the door.

'What the fuck?' Danny yelled, scrambling to get out of the car. 'It's them. It's them... Quick, get out. Now, Smiler, move it! The bastard's one of them. Told you we wasn't safe anywhere. They must have topped that Rita bloke. Come on, man, move it.'

'It's all right, don't panic. It's me.' Robert threw the holdall onto the floor of the front seat. 'Danny, it's all right - it's me.'

But Danny wasn't listening. As Robert grabbed the car door handle in an attempt to keep it shut, Danny, in a state of panic, found strength he never knew he had, pushing the door open, and ripping one of Robert's nails off in the process. Shrugging Smiler off as he grabbed for his cardigan, he was out of the car and bolting for the exit before either of them could do anything.

'Shit!' Robert said. 'I should have told him what I was going to do, but never gave it a thought.'

'We better get after him,' Smiler said, pulling the door shut.

Robert jumped into the car. 'Which way did he go?'

'Actually, changed me mind. Let the scruffy fucker go, 'cos I'm not really bothered. He stinks worse than Tiny does when he's been out in the rain.'

'Smiler!'

'What?'

Robert glared at him.

'OK… OK… He turned left.'

Robert drove out of the petrol station. 'Can you see him?'

Smiler rose up in his seat and, leaning forward, peered out the front window. 'Not yet.'

'He must have turned off. But which way?'

'Left, go left. Here, this one,' Smiler almost shouted. 'He's gone left, I can fucking well smell him.'

Pulling a face at Smiler in the rear view mirror, Robert spun the wheel, just missing an old man and his black-and-white Jack Russell as they stepped off the path. Yelling, 'Sorry!' and sucking his little finger with the missing nail, he drove on down a tree-lined avenue with large houses on each side. 'Any sign yet?'

'No. Keep moving.'

'Shit. We've got to find him before they do.'

'There he is! Just beside that red car, about seven houses down.'

'OK… Got him.'

Robert pressed the accelerator. A moment later, he was spinning in front of the red car and blocking the road off. They both jumped out of the car, Smiler running round the back while Robert ran around the front end, and they managed to trap Danny between them.

Feeling like a cornered rat with no way out, Danny yelled at them, 'Fuck off!'

'Danny.' Robert held his hands up in a placating gesture. 'Please, we mean you no harm. Just get back in the car.'

'No fucking way.'

'Please. I already told you, things will be better explained when we get there. I can talk all day and there'll still be gaps, but the woman we're going to meet, she knows it all.'

'Who the fuck are you?' Danny was beginning to calm down and, thinking straight, he guessed rightly that Robert was Rita. Still, he thought, it had been a hell of a shock, a strange bloke trying to get into the car.

'You're a freak.' He spat the words at Robert before he could answer him. 'And you're fucking well one of them…gotta be.' He turned to Smiler. 'And you an' all, bunch of fucking freaks.'

'Take that back, fucking stinky bastard,' Smiler shouted at him.

Robert said calmly, 'I'm Rita… And I'm Robert, sometimes Rob. I make no excuses for either. It's the way I came.'

It was Robert's voice and what he'd said that stopped Danny in his tracks. For a moment, he felt ashamed of what he'd yelled at him. He had an uncle, a big hairy biker, who cross-dressed. When the family had found out, they'd disowned him, and forbidden Danny ever to see the uncle, in case he caught it. Silly fools.

But the fear of everything that had happened overcame his shame. Because he just couldn't fathom out who the hell was telling the truth.

'It means nowt. You're part of them.'

'No, we're not,' Smiler snapped.

'Piss off, freak!'

'No, we aren't Danny. We are a part of what has happened to you, yes, but both Smiler and I are also the victims - along with a whole lot of other people. Please listen. It's time for you to start believing. Trust me… We're your friends.'

Danny sighed. 'My friends are dead.'

'I know, Danny, but we're your new friends. We are also part of something great and good, something special, something that is fighting back.' He held out his hand. 'We want you to be a part of that, Danny… Come on, please get in the car. I promise shortly you'll understand everything.'

Danny stared at Robert's extended hand. Again, he didn't know what to think. This Robert bloke tells a convincing tale, but confusion has become an everyday thing.

To trust them or not?

He looked up into Robert's eyes for a moment, and made a decision. Slowly he walked around the car, and got back in his seat. Smiler opened the window, but threw Danny a quick smile when he saw Robert frowning at him in the mirror. Giving a shrug, he wound it back up to halfway.

PART TWO

NORFOLK
1110 AD

'It is time now for me to head north, alone,' Godric said to his old friend. 'The book is to be taken to a safe place, where in the future, when there are many more in our band, and the power begins to shift because good men refuse to be idle, the wrongs of many can be put right.'

His friend nodded. Looking into Godric's clear grey eyes beneath his bushy brows, he felt honoured to be considered friend by such a brave and kind man.

'When will you go?'

'Soon. First I must go to Lindisfarne, and spend some time there with the monks, then I will retire to a beautiful remote spot near the river at Finchale.'

'I will miss you, old friend.'

'We have had many adventures, seen places that most won't ever see in their lifetimes,' Godric replied. 'But this final adventure I must do alone. The book must be preserved for future generations so they will finally know who the real tyrants are, and hopefully be in a position to let the world know.'

His friend rose and held out his hand. 'It has been an honour to know you, Godric.'

'And you too.'

Closing the door behind his friend, Godric, destined to become Saint Godric, picked up the book, still wrapped in the horsehair blanket, and held it to his chest.

CHAPTER THIRTY-FIVE
Present Day

The lift door opened, and a young woman texting on her phone stepped in. She had dark hair that much Mike saw in the very brief glance he gave her. He swallowed hard and kept his eyes on the ground, wondering if it was his ever-so-lovely sister Lovilla, perhaps on her way back up to torment him again. The swift look he'd taken had not been enough to tell who she was. Mike did not believe in lifting his hands to hit a woman, he found the process disgusting and cowardly. But there were exceptions to every rule, and if this so-called sister of his came between him and his freedom, then she would get it, good and proper.

Both Mike and Ella heaved a sigh of relief a moment later when, after completely ignoring them as if they didn't even exist, the woman stepped out at the next floor and, still texting walked along the corridor. They both thanked God there was no one waiting to get in.

'Next stop, the basement,' Ella said, watching the numbers tick over on the lift door and bracing herself.

'Yep… Can't believe we've made it this far.' Staring at the doors, he shook his head.

His stare had become so intent that Ella pictured him ripping the doors open and running as fast as he could to get away from here, with herself tearing after him.

At last, after what seemed an age with the lift pausing at every floor, they reached the basement. Carefully holding her arm out to stop Mike from stepping out first, just in case, she reasoned to herself, Ella looked around. 'OK,' she said, 'it's clear, follow me. And don't make any sudden moves like trying to make a dash for it. Trust me, it wont work. The guards will be on your back in seconds.'

Nodding at her and taking a deep breath, Mike strolled casually out of the lift behind Ella.

He would take his time. Ella was right. We've come this far, get a grip and don't do anything to spoil it, he thought, because one way or another I will be back, and there'll be big payback coming to these bastards all right. Mark my words, they are without doubt going to be sorted. Callous inhuman bastards!

Unable to believe their luck, and still keeping up the pretence of not knowing each other, they walked along the basement corridor. It was grey and dismal down here, with peeling paint and patches of missing wallpaper showing patches of mould in places. No one cared what surrounded the peasants, or really what sort of squalor they lived in. They were, after all, only peasants. And the workers in from the town were paid good enough wages not to complain about the state of the place. After all, they didn't have to sleep here, and those that did rarely spoke to a townie. Not that a lot of them could speak

English. Those that could, kept their heads down, just about ignoring everyone, and got on with their work.

They moved on past the noisy kitchen. Even though the door was closed, the sound of yelling orders, banging pots and pans and dropped crockery seeped into the corridor. With Ella praying that no one was out on a ciggie break, or just having a few minutes away from the madness, they made it outside to the bike sheds.

'OK, pick one bike, but casual like, as if it's yours. Remember the cameras… And keep your head down,' Ella said, jumping on her own bike, which was in a dark corner away from the security cameras. She couldn't risk being seen on camera, riding out of the place with Mike as if they were together.

'Go out the front, turn left and keep going. I'll have to go through the woods, then through the field. I'll catch up with you in five.'

Before Mike could even nod, she was off in the opposite direction and, in moments, out of sight. Shrugging, he jumped on a green bike that looked the worse for wear, but had the best tyres of the half-dozen bikes that were there. The last thing he needed, a few yards from the place, was a puncture. Trying to look as if he belonged, and it was perfectly normal for him to be there, he rode out the way she had told him. True to her word, five minutes later Ella came out of a cornfield full of red poppies to ride alongside him.

Not much later, after a few hairy moments when two or three cars came up behind them, they were on the outskirts of Norwich. Mike pedalled behind Ella. They looked like nothing more than a couple out for a bike ride since, a mile or so back, Mike had got rid of the waiter's jacket and tie, and rolled his sleeves up.

Still amazed that they had got away with it so far, they stopped when Ella pulled up outside a large Victorian house. Mike heaved a sigh of relief.

'This is it,' she said, dismounting. 'Oh, by the way - you should be prepared. A few surprises waiting for you.'

Mike raised his eyebrows. Surprises! Hah... Tell me another!

The words had barely left her mouth when a car pulled up beside them. Warily, Mike looked around for a weapon.

For fuck's sake, this flaming close!

It'll have to be the bike, nothing else lying about, he was thinking. He was preparing to pick the bike up and bounce it off the head of anyone who stepped out of the car, when one of the back doors burst open and a grinning Smiler jumped out.

'Mike!' he yelled, hurrying round the side of the car, a first time actual huge-sized grin on his face.

Amazed, Mike, who had the bike up in midair, froze, then quickly put the bike down when Smiler reached him.

'Looking good, kid,' Mike grinned.

For a brief moment there was a slight awkwardness between them neither of them knowing quite what to do then Mike opened his arms and they hugged. Smiler dashed tears out of his eyes thinking, this is getting to be a habit.

Getting out of the car, Danny leaned his back against it and, with a stubborn look on his face, glared at them and watched everything with his arms folded across his chest. Robert walked over to Mike and Smiler. He was holding his right hand with his left. 'Sorry, can't shake, but I'm Robert, and this is Danny.'

Mike nearly did a double-take when he looked at Danny. 'You!'

'You've met?' Robert asked with raised eyebrows.

'Oh yes… It's a long story.' He turned back to Danny. 'What the hell are you of all people doing here?'

Danny shrugged. 'You tell me!'

'Unbelievable.'

'Shall we go inside?' Ella said, looking around, hoping that they weren't drawing attention to themselves. Thankfully the back street was empty, not even a parked car the whole length of it. She went on, 'There's people been waiting for to see you all.' She smiled at Danny. Grim-faced and still wary of everything and everybody, he just looked at her, no smile, nothing.

'OK,' Mike replied, his arm across Smiler's shoulder, thinking with a touch of amazement just how far Smiler had come to even allow this kind of contact, never mind the hug.

With Ella in the lead, Smiler and Mike side by side and Robert and Danny behind, they all went into the house.

When Aunt May had said hello to a very surprised Mike, who had swept her up in a bear hug, and she had shared the same hug with Smiler, she turned to Danny and held out her hand. 'Hello Danny. You must be dying to see Shelly.'

'Not really.' He shrugged, not admitting that, deep inside, he really wanted nothing more than to hold Shelly in his arms, and had done since this whole business started, no matter how much he denied it. *And just who the hell is this old woman?*

Aunt May smiled in a knowing way and turned to Coral, who had gone for Shelly and was just coming back into the room, while Ella was coming in from the kitchen with the first aid tin to see to Robert's finger. Coral looked from Ella to Aunt May, a shocked look on her face. ' She's gone.'

'No way!' Ella looked at Aunt May.

'I've searched everywhere,' Coral said. 'And she's not here.'

For a moment there was silence, then Danny shouted, 'I knew it! It's all a fucking farce to get me to come. You're all part of them... I knew it... Bastards!'

'No, Danny,' Ella said.

'Suicidal, my fucking arse she is. Shelly never was here, and she's not the suicidal type anyhow. All a bunch of fucking lies... You're with them, aren't you?' Frantically he looked around for an escape route.

'Ask yourself why, fucking idiot? Why would anyone go to all of this just to get to you?' Smiler asked.

'Fuck off, you,' Danny snapped at him. 'You're the icing on the cake. Look at your fucking face, man. What sort of fucking blow job idiot carves a smile on his face?'

'Fuck off yourself.' Smiler raised his fists. 'And take a whiff of yourself, stinky bastard.'

Although in a sense Mike agreed with what some of what Smiler had said, because Danny certainly stank, he frowned at Smiler's tone. What was up with these two?

Aunt May quickly moved forward, also throwing a frown at Smiler as she did so.

'Danny, please. What will it take for you to believe us?'

Danny shrugged, and said to Aunt May, 'You don't know half of what's gone on. They were the start of it, him and another friggin' copper.' He waved his hand at Mike. 'Accused me of murdering me mate's girlfriend. They even got me locked up. Then I ended up in a fucking…pardon me…drug factory, with a bunch of lunatics. And… And… My best friend is dead. Shelly…well, Shelly, you said she was here and she's not. And no one cares, got no friends, got nobody, 'cos they all think I murdered Alicia.'

Aunt May sighed. 'Danny, I'm so sorry for your loss, and every-thing that's happened to you. But please, give us a chance. I assure you, with all my heart we are not part of them, as you like to call the families.'

Cutting her off, Danny went on, 'You still don't understand, do you? I've got nobody… What the hell am I supposed to believe?' he implored them as he started to sob. 'It's too much…Too much. I can't take anymore. '

He couldn't go on. Everything came crashing around him, and he fell to his knees. They all took a step towards him, but Smiler got there first.

Taking a deep breath, and hesitating ever so slightly, Smiler put his hand on Danny's shoulder. He felt the stiffness there, and knew some of the pain Danny was going through. 'Danny,' he said. 'Let me help you.'

Danny froze.

'Please Danny.'

Aunt May and Mike looked at each other, and shared the briefest of smiles.

CHAPTER THIRTY-SIX

Shelly stared straight ahead in the car. Although late afternoon, the sun was bright, and she took in every house, tree and garden that they passed, plus the names of the streets, ensuring the route back was wired into her brain. Her memory of maps and places had always been good, and had served her before in sticky situations.

And now it was just open road. Green fields, a lot of cows, even more sheep.

Her heart kept skipping beats, because she knew exactly which hell they would take her to. The drug sheds first, and put her to work immediately. Once in there, there was no escape, nowhere to hide or run to. The guards patrolled the drug sheds with guns and whips, watching, all the time watching. And because her hair was now blonde, instead of black, she probably wouldn't see the Leader's bed tonight, but that was only just probably.

'The bastard,' she muttered, unable to stop herself.

'Sorry?'

'Nothing, babes.' She gave him a cheery smile, and threw him an air kiss, playing the blonde bimbo to the hilt, before turning back to the window.

He smiled, his dimples deepening.

Inwardly, she sighed. Am I doing the right thing?

Because once the Leader finds out that a newbie is in, he'll deffo want to taste the wares, either tonight or tomorrow night.

And that would be good, a relief, she tried to convince herself.

Get it over and done with right off, before the bastards started plying her with drugs. Because the truth of the matter was, she didn't really know how long she would be able to resist, how long it would be before she stopped palming them and swallowed the lot.

Also, this creep's fucking aftershave is vile!

'So, babes, how far away is this place?' she asked, turning slightly in her seat and giving him a seductive smile.

'Couple of miles.' He smiled back at her. 'Won't be long now. Trust me, you're gonna love it.' His smile changed to a grin as he turned the radio on full and blasted Lady Gaga, giving no more opportunity for small talk.

A few minutes later they pulled up outside a large set of heavy-looking metal gates. The high stone wall to her left looked like it went on forever, and large trees gave no chance of seeing anything that was in there.

'Here we go,' he muttered, turning the radio off.

She gripped the edge of her seat to stop herself from freaking out. The place was the exact double of the monastery. Even before she saw the rest of it, she knew what was coming.

Taking a gadget out of his pocket, he pressed a button on it and the gates opened.

As he drove through, and the gates started to close behind them, Shelly steeled herself. This was it. She'd come this far, and she would go through with it.

No turning back now.

CHAPTER THIRTY-SEVEN

Kristina and Patrick's journey to Norwich was uneventful, following the same route taken a few hours earlier by Aunt May and Brother David. Now, scratching his beard and looking at the house numbers, Patrick slowly drove down the back street. They had made good time except for a twenty-mile zone of fifty only on the motorway, in which Patrick had fretted, declaring what he would do if he ever caught the red cone man in person.

'I mean,' he'd said more than once, 'who the hell is he? Have you ever seen him? 'Cos I haven't. You go to bed, no cones. You wake up the next morning, and they're all over the bloody place. I reckon, whoever he is, he should be shot. Or at the very least, put in the tower so the birds can peck his eyes out. No more cones, eh?'

Kristina had laughed at the image. Patrick had turned out to be a natural comedian with a very dry wit, and cracked jokes all the way down. She'd laughed even more when they had pulled in at a garage and Patrick had gone in for some coffees. He'd come out, tripped over, and the coffees and doughnuts had flown up into the air, somersaulted, then come back down and splashed all over him. A man on his way into the garage got splashed, but he laughed louder than Kristina.

At last, satisfied that he had the right house, they pulled up close to the gate and got out of the car. Patrick was about to open the gate when it was pulled open from the other side, and a young man ran out.

'Danny! Kristina said, slightly amazed that he would be here of all places.

'You? Oh God, not another one!' he yelled, spotting her.

'Stop him,' Ella screamed, running out after him, followed by Mike and Coral.

Reacting quickly, Patrick grabbed for Danny's middle and spun round with him just as Mike reached them.

'Get off me,' Danny yelled. 'Fuck off.' He struggled with Patrick, but when Mike joined in, he knew he had no chance. Deflated, he stopped struggling.

'Phew,' Patrick said. 'You're ripe, son.'

'Fuck off, old goat.'

Coral shot Patrick a sorry look. He smiled. 'No problem Coral love. And may I say, you're looking as lovely as ever, my dear.'

'Thank you, Patrick, and the same back... Come on, Danny. Come inside and I'll get you some fresh clothes.'

Danny glared at her. It isn't my fault that I stink, no one's given me the chance to change clothes, he thought, then looked at them all. No chance of ever getting away from here either.

Fucking surrounded.

When is it all gonna end?

Again filled with despair, and actually having listened to the things Smiler had been saying to him when everyone had left the room and left them alone to talk, he gave in. Not that he'd planned to go far. He just really needed some time to clear his head, and get used to the fact that Smiler seemed an OK kind of guy, who had been to hell and back himself, and was coping in his own way.

In fact the last thing he'd said, before they all came back, was, 'It gets a tiny bit better every day.'

'All right,' he declared. 'But I want some explanations about every fucking thing that's gone on. And why the fuck I've been tossed from pillar to post for the last few weeks. As well as practically being accused of everything under the fucking sun.' He glared at Mike and Kristina in turn. 'And you two!'

'You'll get them, Danny,' Ella said. 'I promise you, we've just been waiting to get everyone together.'

'OK, but I want the truth this time.'

'Don't we all,' Mike said.

Ignoring him, Danny went on, 'I mean it. Not gonna be fobbed off with a load of rubbish this time… I want to know why two of my best friends are dead, why you told me Shelly was here when she's not, and just who the fuck Them are. And you all know who I mean when I say Them! Don't you! 'Cos I know this is all down to Them. And you're all fucking well in on it. In fact, want to know something?

I'm fucking sick of asking!'

'Take him in, Coral. I won't be long, just need to...' Mike said, missing her nod, because his eyes were for Kristina only, and hers for him.

When they had all gone in, Kristina moved towards Mike. Suddenly his arms were wrapped around her. After a moment, he looked deep into her eyes and said, 'Why did we let it end, Kristina? How could we have been so, so stupid?'

Kristina shook her head. 'I don't know, Mike. One of those things, I suppose...' She shrugged. 'Shit happens. But now,' she smiled up at him, 'now I feel like I've finally come home.'

'There's a lot of talking to be done, Kristina. And a lot of listening, with nothing but hard dangerous work ahead... Our own business, though!' He smiled.

'On hold, Mike.'

She smiled up at him, they kissed, then hand in hand followed the others into the house.

Half an hour later, Mike sat with one arm around Aunt May, the other around Kristina, with Smiler next to Aunt May, and Ella taking a photograph. 'Put your arm around Aunt May, Smiler,' she urged him. For the briefest of moments he hesitated, then with a smile he put his arm around Aunt May. She leaned in and rested her head on his shoulder. Smiler felt as if his heart would burst.

Mike had never been so happy for the longest time. He was with everyone he loved. For this brief calm before the storm, it was as if the families didn't exist, and life was sweet.

A few minutes later Brother David, who had spent most of the day in prayer until Mike popped up to see him for a quick catch up, arrived downstairs to join them, taking care to avoid looking at Coral and keeping as far away from her as possible. He was followed by Danny, who had showered, shaved and now wore jeans and a blue t-shirt that actually fitted him.

Aunt May stood up. 'OK, time to get down to a few bloody home truths, all.'

When she had finally finished speaking, she was met with stunned silence for a moment. Until Danny, the first one to find his voice, blurted, 'So basically, 'cos a whole bunch of fucking…sorry.' He shot a quick smile at Aunt May. 'Like I said, because of these people's greed, we're all in the mess that we're in now?'

'Basically yes, that and the love of power.'

'Well, count me in, whatever you've got planned, OK? But in the meantime, what about Shelly?'

CHAPTER THIRTY-EIGHT

Shelly thought she was seeing things when the gates closed behind her. Feeling as if she'd been transported back to the monastery near Berwick she stared around her, fear flooding through her body the closer to the building that they got.

Jesus Christ! It is a carbon copy of the monastery.

Can't do this.

No way!

Keep calm. Turning her face to the window so that he couldn't see, she took a couple of deep breaths.

No backing out now

'What, er…is it a hotel?' she asked, searching her mind for his name, then remembering he'd never actually given it.

'Sort of,' he replied, with a sarcastic smile. 'Trust me, you're gonna really love it here.'

'Thought you were just picking some gear up?

'Yeah, but we gotta socialise a bit.' He put his hand on her knee and squeezed. 'Know what I mean?'

Shelly knew what he meant all right, and at this moment it was all she could do to keep herself from latching tightly onto his throat. Determined to see it through, she kept telling herself to be calm. One way or another, preferably before tonight was over, she would see her day with the bastard.

He brought the car to a stop close to the main door and, like a gentleman introducing a lady to her new home, hurried around the car and opened the door with a flourish.

Pretending not to realise that the tight grip he had on her arm as they walked to the door was to stop her from running away, she smiled innocently up at him as the door opened.

His grip tightened, as she'd guessed it would. Playing along, she started to struggle and glared at him.

'Let go, you're hurting me.'

'Can't do that, sorry. Not until I hand you over.'

God! she thought, remembering the monastery, do they all go through a fucking induction course?

'What do you mean, hand me over?' She struggled harder. Before he had a chance to answer her, the heavy oak-panelled door opened, and a tall, broad-shouldered man reached out his hand and grabbed her other arm.

'Hello,' he said. 'Welcome.'

'No!' Shelly screamed. 'Let me go!'

'Bye,' the man who had brought her said, a big dimpled smile on his face as he turned back to the car. He was practically clapping his hands in delight. Before the night was over, he hoped to bring in at least another two willing victims.

The big man with the bald head dragged her through the door then, keeping hold of her with an iron grip, he locked the door with his other hand. Pretending to be overawed by everything that was happening, not that it took too much pretence, Shelly stared around at her surroundings. It was so much like the monastery that it was practically unbelievable, right down to the tiniest detail. The whole set up freaked her out. Silently, facing away from the guard, she took some more deep breaths, wondering if they were doing any good. She was still in a state of panic, and the tight lid she had on it kept slipping.

Her mind, though, was racing. This must be the new guy drafted in to take the place of the last guard I injected. A small glimmer of satisfaction drifted through her. He had been a nasty bastard all right, and deserved what he'd got.

'Move it,' the new guard said.

'No thank you, mate. If you're up to kinky stuff in here, you picked the wrong girl. I'm off. ' She turned towards the door, but he still had tight hold of her.

'You're not going anywhere.'

'I am so!' She made a big show of struggling with him, even though she knew it was useless. She had to keep up the pretence at all cost.

Ignoring her protests and keeping tight hold of her, he answered his ringing mobile. After a moment he said, 'OK, got it.'

'No. Get your fucking paws off me.' She slapped his face hard.

He smiled at her. The bastard hasn't even blinked, Shelly thought, a tingle of fear running up her spine.

'Come with me, girl, and you'll get what you came for all right.' With hardly any effort, he dragged her to a doorway that she knew just had to lead off to half a dozen rooms kept for the newbies until, after only a few days, they became totally addicted. Then they were forced to sleep in the sheds with the rest of the workers.

The door opened just before they reached it and another guard stepped in.

Shit! she thought, for God's sake, please, please don't let the freak recognize me.

She put her head down, but she could feel his eyes boring into her. She knew it was now or never. Her fingers twisted the lid of the insulin pen in her pocket, then flicked it off with her thumb. She turned the top until it reached the very end. She'd practised this over and over and, though still terrified that the very fine needle might snap, she was even more terrified that this lecherous bastard might recognize her.

'Look at me,' he demanded.

Poised for action, and trying hard to keep a look of revulsion on her face, she lifted her head.

'Hmm, the hair colour's all wrong.' He paused for a moment studying her.

Shelly's heart felt as if it would burst. He knows it's me. Shit!

'But now and again he doesn't mind a change.'

Oh my God thank you. Shelly thought, her heart easing. He doesn't know it's me.

'You'll do for tonight's entertainment.'

'For what?' she yelled, continuing to play the game. 'And get your hands off me, creep, or I'll call the police. Fucking pervert.'

He laughed out loud. Insults were two a penny, and he'd heard the lot. They were all of them, without exception, very, very sorry later. Slowly he studied her face, wondering briefly if he'd seen her somewhere before.

'I'll take her, shall I?' the first guard said, breaking the spell.

'Why, what you after, like?' The original guard looked at him suspiciously.

'Nothing. Just thought I'd save you the trek.'

'I'll take her.'

He turned, his grip tightening on her arm and, heart pounding again, Shelly deciding that plan A was out the window. It had been stupid, anyhow. No way would she have been able to inject this gorilla in front of the Leader, then get away with attacking the Leader. Wonder Woman she definitely wasn't. It was now or never, though. New plan - sort the gorilla, then go for the Leader, supposing she had to get into bed with the bastard.

'Come on,' he said, without looking at her.

Playing along, Shelly dug her heels in, but the strength he possessed was way above normal, and she may as well have been a fly batting against a pane of glass trying to be free.

The door slammed behind them, and quickly Shelly pulled her insulin pen out. What worked before will work again, she reasoned as, pretending to trip, she used his strength to pull her over and pressed the plunger, injecting the full dose into the top of his leg.

In moments, he crumbled. Suspecting nothing, he stared at her, puzzlement in his eyes just before they closed.

The door opened and Shelly jumped up, snatching the second pen out of her pocket. She was ready to do it again, to whoever came through the door.

CHAPTER THIRTY-NINE

'You sure you've searched everywhere?' Ella asked, trying to keep the worry out of her voice and failing miserably.

'She's gone looking for them, hasn't she,' Coral stated. 'Check the fridge for her insulin pens.'

Seeing as he was the closest, Smiler jumped up and went into the kitchen. A few moments later, he was back. 'No sign of any insulin pens in there.'

Mike frowned. 'Where do you think she's gone?'

'I know where she's gone.' Coral replied. 'She's gone looking for the Leader.'

Mike raised his eyebrows.

'Ah, Mike. You don't know, do you, that the other night she had the guts to inject one of the Leader's guards with insulin.'

'Hmm, well done her.'

The rest of them nodded.

'She what?' Brother David said in awe.

'She--'

'Yes, I know what you said... Wow, brave girl.'

Danny smiled at everyone. Way to go, Shelly, he was thinking. For the first time in weeks, his heart felt just that little bit lighter, until Aunt May brought him crashing back down.

'You do all realise she bloody well might not be coming back.'

Every pair of eyes turned to Danny. Looking back at them, he shook his head and, even knowing the danger she had put herself in, said, 'She will… I know she will.'

CHAPTER FORTY

Shelly held the pen like a spear just above her right shoulder. The first guard lay perfectly still at her feet, apart from his left foot which was twitching ever so slightly. Her hands were trembling, but she'd done what she had set out to do.

Although she knew it wasn't over yet.

And now the door was slowly opening and creaking, just like the door in that other hell had creaked, and the other guard stepped through.

Without hesitation, Shelly threw herself at him.

'No, Shelly, stop,' he yelled, as the needle made contact with his shoulder. 'You don't understand, I'm on your side.'

'Liar!' she screamed, pressing the plunger. 'No one's on my side, least of all you... Die!'

He twisted away from her and grabbed her arm then, pushing her away from him, he quickly pulled the pen out of his shoulder. Seeing that it was empty, he stared at her in horror.

'Die, bastard, die for everything you've ever done.'

He shook his head, his face white with shock. 'Shelly, you don't understand.'

'Ha! I understand all right, and you're dead, mate. Just like him. Die, you bastard, make the world a better place.'

A moment later he felt cold liquid run down his arm. He gasped, and Shelly, thinking it was his last breath, smiled.

He smiled back at her as he said, 'The needle must have stuck in the seam of my jacket.'

Shelly's face dropped. Frantically she looked around for an escape route. Get out, get out, her mind was screaming at her.

'It's all right, Shelly, I'm on your side,' he repeated, slowly so it would penetrate the fear and doubt he could see on her face, and the panic as he saw her reach into her pocket.

How many needles has she got in there? he wondered. He'd been lucky once!

'Please, please, Shelly, you've got to believe me. How do you think I know your name? Take time, think hard. Have you ever seen me before, anywhere?'

'What?' She paused for a moment. It hadn't occurred to her until he mentioned it that he had been calling her by her name. 'But how…How can I….' She gestured with her hand to the now lifeless body on the floor. 'You…you look just like him, it takes a certain kind of person to do what he does.' She shook her head.

'Shelly.'

'No. I don't believe you.'

'You haven't got a choice.' He went on quickly, 'I'm part of Aunt

May's set up, Shelly, for fuck's sake, not this lot. Now quick, we've got to move him before anyone comes along. There's no one else we can trust in here. And you are just going to have to trust me, girl…I'm all you've got.'

Still unsure, she stared at him.

Reaching down, he grabbed the guard's arms and started pulling him down the corridor. 'Open the third door down, quickly.'

Making her mind up - like he said, she thought, there's no one else - she ran ahead of him and opened the door wide, and he pulled the guard through. Straightening up, he looked at Shelly and said, 'I'm Mitch by the way, short for Mitchell. And I know you're Shelly, that phone call was from Ella.'

Shelly looked at him. Should she trust him or not? He knew all the right names, but that could be a cover. He could be working for both sides. 'Help!' she wanted to yell, but help would never come. Not in here, the home of the damned.

'OK,' she said after a moment, knowing that she had no choice and had to trust him. 'What now?'

He looked around the small room. It was a library with one narrow window on the far side. The walls were lined with books. Some of them, he knew, were very rare, and the outside world thought they were lost forever. The Leader, cursed with insomnia, used the library mostly in the middle of the night, sometimes disturbing a slave's sleep to read to him. Next to the window there was a spiral staircase that led up to the Leader's bedroom.

'Ah, I know. Quickly, while I pull him over to the staircase, grab something heavy.'

Obeying, though not having a clue what he was going to do, Shelly searched the room with her eyes. Spotting what looked like a very heavy candlestick on the desk she ran over, grabbed it up and met him at the staircase.

'What now?'

'Now we're gonna have to make it look like an accident, as much as we can.'

She frowned. 'How?'

'Well, let's just say he fell down the stairs and hit his head just here. It's possible, people fall downstairs everyday, don't they?' He took the brass candlestick from her, raised it above his own head and brought it crashing down on the guard's head, leaving a huge indent in his skull.

Shelly flinched, then watched as he placed the guard to look like he'd fallen down the stairs and caved his head in on the corner of the staircase.

Stepping back, he looked at the body, studied the angle of the fall from all directions then, nodding his satisfaction, he then turned to Shelly. 'OK, it's your call. You either get out of here as if you've never been, or you carry on with what you came to do. Make your mind up while I wash this.'

Taking the candlestick into the small toilet and washroom off the library, he ran the tap until the water was scalding hot, then washed the tiny fragments of bone, flesh and spots of blood off the candlestick, making sure that it was spotless as he dried it.

Returning it to its place, he said to Shelly, 'Well?'

Shelly lifted her head, and with a look of pure determination said, 'I came here to do something, and I'm not going until it's finished, one way or another. I won't be happy until I see this hell hole burnt to the ground, and those bastards with it.'

He nodded. 'OK, just let me finish up here.'

Walking over to the body, he lifted the head up and with both hands squeezed the flesh on each side of the wound, draining as much blood out as he could.

'What the...?'

'Last thing we want is anyone to think that he was dead before he hit his head.'

Shelly swallowed hard. 'I suppose so.'

He smiled. 'Right. I suggest I take you into his room, see if he wants you.'

Shelly shivered, remembering the last time she'd been in the Leader's bedroom.

'You sure about this?' Mitch asked her.

'Yes… No… Yes.' Holding her head high, the last 'yes' was spoken with great determination.

He shrugged. 'But only if you're certain, girl. Me, I would get the hell outta here now if I was you.'

She shook her head adamantly. 'No.'

'OK, but you know there isn't a lot I can do except wait outside the door to help you if you succeed.'

'If I succeed, what will the plan be then?'

'Then we let these poor bastards go. Might have to kill some of the hired guns first, but I think I'll be able to talk them round. What would be the point of staying, unless one of those jerks wanted to set themselves up as the kingpin? Doubt it, though. The best thing is to get outta here and hope they're never traced again.'

'What if they want to kill those in the drug sheds, so that they will never be recognised?'

'We'll cross that when we come to it… For now?' He raised one eyebrow in a question.

'I'm ready,' she replied, the determination flooding back into her eyes. 'Take me in.'

CHAPTER FORTY-ONE

Kirill Tarasov watched from the veranda of his apartment as family members started leaving for their places of origin. Five helicopters waited in the hotel heliport. Two had already left. One of those had been transporting his daughter and son home.

Which is just as well, he thought, his hands squeezing the cushion from the chair at his side. He was staying on for another few days. He had a meeting scheduled with a very important woman tomorrow.

And now as he watched two other helicopters take to the sky, his thoughts were once again focused on the only woman he had ever in his whole life loved.

Why, he asked himself, what had been so different about her that she stood out from countless other women around the world?

How has she managed to stay hidden this long?

True, I gave up the search years ago.

But still rather amazing that with all my resources, I still couldn't find her.

He turned away from the view and went inside. A small brandy was needed before he paid a visit to his illegal son. A visit he had been putting off for the last couple of hours, because he truly didn't know what to do, and this was a situation he hated. He liked to be in charge, was used to being in charge. He drank the brandy down in one quick angry gulp.

Making his way upstairs, he opened the door to the locked room. Stepping inside, he blinked twice as his brain caught up with his eyes. The bed was empty, and the handcuffs were lying in the middle of the white sheet.

'Where the hell...?' he muttered, going over to the bed in disbelief.

Ten minutes later he was stamping back and forth in front of seven agents, waving his arms in the air, and demanding over and over how Mike Yorke had managed to escape from a locked room while handcuffed to a bed.

'You.' He swung round and addressed Josh Millar. 'Where the fuck have you been all day, you must have seen something?'

Keeping his head down, Josh said, 'No, sir. We've been busy getting people onto the helicopters.'

'You, then.' He pointed to a short, balding man standing next to Stone. 'I thought you were in charge of the security cameras.'

'Yes, sir, but nothing unusual was noted.'

'Go through them again. And again, until you find something. It must be there on tape.'

'Yes, sir.' He turned and headed upstairs, followed by the agent who had been standing at the other end.

'Fucking useless, the lot of you. What the fuck are we paying you for, when a man chained to a bed actually escapes, and no one sees him go? Impossible. It has to be an inside job.'

'Sir, we searched the grounds,' Agent Millar said, 'as soon as we found out and…nothing.'

'It's an inside job. He's had help. Got to have had. Do your fucking job and find out who. Bring his…or her...head to me, or else I'll have all of yours, every fucking one of you.'

The agents scattered to begin the search again, knowing that Tarasov was quite capable of carrying out his threat.

CHAPTER FORTY-TWO

Shelly followed Mitch as he left the lift and strode down the corridor to the Leader's room. Inside, she was as determined as ever to see it through, though outwardly she appeared nervous. She knew this because her hands were shaking, but knowing the way that things were run around here, she reasoned that a show of nerves wasn't a bad thing. To appear too cocky in any way would only anger the bastard.

Outside the door, Mitch whispered, 'Last chance to back out. I can still get you away from here, without anyone ever knowing you were here. Don't worry about that jerk who brought you in, he'll have forgotten about you already.' He put his hand on her shoulder. 'Really, Shelly, you don't have to do this.'

Shelly took a deep breath, pursed her lips and took a step forward.

Taking that as her answer, Mitch knocked on the door.

'Come,' they both heard, a second later.

Mitch turned the handle and they both went inside. The Leader was lying stretched out on a queen-size bed, white silk sheets and red velvet hangings tied back with golden ropes. He was naked and lying on his stomach. Two slave girls, one at each side of him, were massaging his back. The look on his face was that of a man who had spent forever frowning at people.

'Ah, a newbie.' He grinned and Shelly felt sick inside.

'Come here, girl, stand in front of me.'

Shelly moved forward, her hands in her pockets. With her thumb and finger she started to twist the top of the pen.

'So, girl, you have a name?'

'S…Susan,' Shelly said, knowing she'd nearly made a big mistake, by saying her real name. So far the blonde hair is throwing him off, but if I'd said my real name, he might have looked harder.

Be careful. Think things through beforehand.

What the fuck's the matter with this? She thought, as the lid on the insulin pen was proving to be stubborn.

Beginning to panic, she gripped the lid tighter and twisted. Another wash of panic swept over her as the lid refused to move. Fucking hell. Her heart began to race.

He sat up. 'Go now.' He looked at the slave girls, then at Mitch. 'You as well, out now.'

'Yes, my Leader,' they said in unison as they backed out of the room.

'No!' Shelly said, her eyes wide in horror as she stared at the Leader.

Thinking this was all part of her plan, Mitch left the room.

Feeling trapped the moment she heard the door close behind

them, Shelly backed away, her eyes widening as the Leader got off the bed and stepped towards her.

What the fuck am I gonna do now?

'Take your coat off, Susan… In fact, take everything off.'

She froze, then shook her head.

'You shake your head? What do you think you're here for? Ah, yes. Lured by the offer of free drugs.' He laughed, and it sent a chill through Shelly's bones. 'There's plenty of them. But first, a small thing like payment.'

He was beside her now.

Why the hell did I think I could get away with this?

It was bound to go wrong.

Frantically she twisted the lid on her pen as he drew closer.

CHAPTER FORTY-THREE

'So what we gonna do now?' Danny demanded. 'How we gonna get her outta that hell hole?' He looked around at them all. Some met his eyes, some couldn't. All of them looked worried.

'Oh, for fuck's sake,' he went on. 'You're using her as a scapegoat, aren't you!' He laughed a harsh, heartbreaking laugh as he looked at them. 'And here's me thinking you're the good guys, huh? Wrong again. There's a surprise.'

'No, Danny.' Aunt May rose. 'Nothing of the bloody kind at all. It's the last bloody thing we would do. Shelly has done this entirely off her own back. Do you honestly think we would be so cruel as to send someone in, when there is no hope of ever getting out of the bloody stinking hell hole?'

Seeing his face drop at Aunt May's words, Ella jumped quickly in. 'Mitch is in there, Danny. He'll do his best to talk her out of it, and get her out of there.'

'You just don't have any idea of what really goes on in there, do you? No idea at all.' Danny spoke from his heart, remembering his time in the monastery, remembering all the dead faces of the young people in there, soulless eyes with no hope at all.

'Oh, yes we do,' Coral said, nodding knowingly at him. 'Most of us have been there. Trust me.'

Danny stared at them. 'Really? I...I didn't know...' He looked at the floor for a moment then, lifting his head, he said, 'So what chance do you think she has of getting out of there alive?'

Ah, Danny, Mike was thinking, trust you to ask the impossible question. Because really she has no chance.

Sadly he went into the kitchen for a drink of water. As the glass was filling, his thoughts jumped back to Aunt May. He was still reeling from the fact that she was more or less in charge of all this.

How has she managed to keep it a secret all this time?

And Tony, where the hell does he fit into this jigsaw?

He felt a presence at his side, and looked down to see Aunt May looking up at him.

'Tony is with us, Mike.'

Mike stepped back just as the water flowed over the glass and soaked his hand.

How does she do that? he wondered. Seems like she's always reading my friggin' mind, ever since we were kids. It seemed like she knew what we were up to before we did.

Turning the tap off, he put the glass down and reached for a piece of kitchen roll. All the time his eyes never left Aunt May's.

'Why did you leave me out?'

'It wasn't a question of bloody well leaving you out, Mike... It just wasn't the time to include you.'

'Ah, but it was time to include Tony.'

'His place of work made him a necessity.'

'So you're saying I'm a liability.'

'Far from it, Mike. You're a good man. A very good man, with a heart of gold… And you were always going to be a part of it. But you are also a bloody loose cannon, you always have been. A bit like Shelly, really. We couldn't afford to bring you in until the time was right.'

'And that's now?'

She nodded. Opening her arms, she added, 'I'm worried sick for Shelly. I could do with a bloody big hug, Mike.'

Without hesitation, Mike put his arms around the only mother he had ever known.

'Any idea where the new monastery is?' he asked.

'Yes, we've had our eye on it for a few weeks now. And Mitch is a good man.'

'OK, give me directions, and keep the others off my back.'

'Mike!'

'Gotta help her, Aunt May, you know this.'

'But--'

'No buts, love. Can't leave her to the wolves without at least giving it a try.'

Aunt May gave the directions to Mike, and the door had just closed behind him when Smiler entered the kitchen. His first words on seeing her alone were, 'Where's Mike?'

'He's just popped to the shop. Actually going to buy himself a packet of bloody cigarettes, would you believe it?' Spinning him round, she ushered him towards the sitting room.

'But--'

'No buts, love.' She repeated what Mike had just said to her with a smile.

CHAPTER FORTY-FOUR

Tony left the pet shop in Soho long after the three men had gone. He'd also let Muriel get off early, more than an hour ago. Ever since then, he'd sat deliberating all that had been said between them.

Like the families, these three, although good men, had their heads in the clouds. Unlike Aunt May, who knew without being told that a seamless transition would take years, the mopping up even longer.

He walked along to the end of the street and looked across at the Palace Theatre. Tony really loved old buildings, and this was one of his favourites.

If only I had time, he thought. Sighing, he turned and headed for the car park.

Reaching his car, a blue Mercedes, he failed to notice the hooded youth until he stepped out in front of him.

'This here your car?' the youth, white, with a face full of spots, demanded with a surly voice.

'What's it to you?'

Tony weighed the youth up. Dressed in the usual get-up of blue hoodie, jeans and white trainers, he was skinny, almost emaciated. Therefore he must have a weapon, or a back-up somewhere close, 'cos this toe rag couldn't skim the skin from a rice pudding.

'Just asking.'

'OK. On your way.'

The sound of Tony's mobile, loud in the enclosed space, startled them both. Always on the ready. Tony made a show of going for his mobile, but instead drew his gun.

The youth, pale to begin with, turned practically chalk white when he saw the gun. Gulping hard he turned and fled, his trainers making a flapping noise. Obviously one of the soles was loose. Reaching the stairs, he never even turned to look back, just headed on down as fast as he could.

'Hmm,' Tony muttered. 'Must have been genuinely interested. Still, can't be too careful in this business.' He got quickly into his car and drove out of the car park, taking care to note everything around him in case the kid came back with a gang.

It wasn't until he was on the motorway that he pulled over in to a rest stop and took his mobile out. He smiled when caller ID said Susan Cleverly.

'Hello lovely, what you got?'

'Hello back... Cox is going to be just fine.'

'Well, thank God for that. We're certainly going to need him in the coming times.'

'Thought you would be pleased. Might be a month or so before he's back on his feet. But I've got plenty armed protection around him, all our own men.'

'Good. I'll be back up your way in a day or two. See you then, and once again…good work.'

'Cheers.'

He closed the phone with a smile, a picture of Susan Cleverly in his mind. Starting the car he headed to Norwich where, no doubt, Mike would be waiting, and wanting answers to questions.

CHAPTER FORTY-FIVE

Shelly stared in horror at the Leader, her heartbeat steadily mounting as her fingers worked frantically on the lid.

Open, please open.

For fuck's sake.

Don't let it all be in vain.

Please, if there is anybody up there...

But her silent pleas went unanswered.

Outside, Mitch paced the corridor. He didn't know what to do. His instinct told him to go in and help the girl, his training told him not to, but to see things through, whatever the outcome.

Torn in half, he turned and punched the wall.

What if, by some miracle, she succeeds? Then it's a whole big problem sorted. If I interfere, and it goes wrong, because he could summon help in a moment, one press of the many emergency buttons around his bedroom, then everything we've worked for all these years could be blown.

Is the risk worth it?

A hell of a lot of people have died for the cause, and it could take years to get someone back in here.

What the hell to do?

The Leader stroked Shelly's arm with his right hand, cupping her chin with his left.

'Don't be frightened, little bird,' he murmured softly, a smirk on his face. 'Let me feel your heart.' Knowing her heart would be beating twice its normal rate, he moved his hand from her chin, ran it over her breast… Suddenly, he froze.

Her jaw dropped a second later when she realised that he had finally recognised her. Shelly panicked.

Pulling the pen out of her pocket, she used her other hand to yank the lid off just as the Leader's hands went round her throat. Immediately he began to squeeze.

'You had me fooled, peasant. But how long did you think it would last?' He shook her, hard. 'Bitch, you know without a doubt what's going to happen now, don't you? Answer me!'

She managed with great difficulty to give a very brief nod, but he could tell in her eyes she knew full well what was going to happen to her now. For a brief moment, dozens of faces flashed across his mind, all of them dead.

'So much sweeter.' He almost whispered his delight. 'Such a pretty, pretty girl.'

One chance only, Shelly thought, as she aimed the pen at his stomach. Feeling the needle meeting its destination, she pressed the plunger, but almost at the same time he swiped it out of her hand. The pen hit the side of the bedpost and fell to the floor, out of Shelly's reach. She began to punch and kick at him, but second by second she could feel herself becoming weaker. His face, full of rage, pressed up against hers. She could smell his foul breath, feel his spit on her face. Slowly the world became darker.

CHAPTER FORTY-SIX

Mike put the directions on top of the dashboard. Fastening the seat-belt, he started the car and drove quickly down the street. Glancing at the directions, he turned right, drove on through two sets of lights, then kept right, and soon he was out into the countryside.

He found the place he wanted, and looked suspiciously at the wrought iron gates, especially at the camera on the left side.

'OK, looks like I'm gonna have to climb over the wall at some point,' he muttered. 'Better get parked.'

Driving on past the cameras and waiting until he was out of range, he turned at the bottom of the road, noting that at twenty-yard intervals there were more cameras. He shot in between two sets of them, and parked the car right up against the wall.

Carefully making sure he was not in any of the cameras sights he got out of the car and, bent double, hurried to the wall. He flattened his back against it and looked left, then right, hoping that because the wall looked quite old, there might be few stones missing from the top.

'No luck there, then, gonna have to do it the fucking hard way. So what's new?'

He found a few handholds, the beauty of stone as opposed to trying to climb a brick wall, and hoisted himself up. In seconds he was up and over. Hastily, he looked around for guard dogs, though there had been none up at the monastery. Either Mr Leader felt secure enough not to need them, or he didn't like them, Mike thought, favouring the latter.

Possibly because no dog worth its salt would like that bastard!

He found himself in a small, dense forest of trees with roots winding their way just below ground, as well as over. He had to watch his step. A broken ankle wasn't going to help anything.

As the trees began to thin out, the building came into view. Mike stopped dead.

'Jesus,' he muttered, staring at the house. 'Impossible. How the hell...?'

Between him and the house was a vast stretch of lawn, where he would be seen as soon as he set foot on it. Then he remembered, if for some insane reason everything panned out to be a carbon copy of the monastery, that at the right side of the house the trees were very much closer, and one section of the building practically touched them. If he came out that way he stood a chance.

Dipping quickly back into the trees, he hurried along and soon came to the spot he wanted. This, if he was right, should be the back of the drug shed.

Slowly he crept around the building until he came to the one and only window. Carefully, he raised his body and risked a quick look inside. A moment was all it took. Shrinking back down, he leaned against the wall and stared into space, a look of deep sadness on his face. The look changed to anger and, steeling himself, he crept along to the door he'd used to get into the monastery near Berwick.

Turning the handle, he pulled, only to find it was locked.

'Damn. Everything in duplicate except Brother Dave.'

It would have to be the window. He looked around for something to put over his hand. Finding nothing, he whipped his jacket off and wrapped it around his hand. Without hesitating, he knocked the pane out. Shaking his jacket to get rid of the glass, he slipped it on and felt through the pane for the key in the lock.

'Thank God,' he whispered when his hand found the key. Turning it, the door slipped silently open.

He went inside, crossed the room and moved into the corridor. Knowing exactly where he wanted to be, he made for the third door.

Mitch was practically hopping from foot to foot, torn about doing the right thing.

'Fuck it.' Suddenly he did the only thing he could, taking a deep breath he kicked the door in, just in time to see Shelly sliding down the Leader's chest.

The Leader looked at him with a scowl. He let go of Shelly, and she dropped the rest of the way to the floor.

Mike entered the library and headed for the staircase, seeing the guard's body halfway across. Reaching the guard, he knelt down and felt for a pulse.

'Stone dead,' he muttered. 'Well, that's one nuisance out of the way. Wonder if Shelly pushed him down the stairs.'

He looked up the staircase. By rights, it should lead to the Leader's bedroom, he thought, stepping over the dead guard's body and putting his foot on the first stair.

Wasting no time, Mitch launched himself across the floor. His fist connecting with the Leader's chin knocked him sideways, but only for a moment. Then he came back, snarling,

Both men started throwing punches. Ignoring the hits he was taking in his ribs, Mitch managed to get his hands around the Leader's head and his thumbs under the Leader's eyes, and pressed hard. Knowing what Mitch was aiming to do and with his eyes bulging out of their sockets, the Leader brought his knee up fast into Mitch's groin. Mitch gasped, and let go of him.

'Bastard!' the Leader screamed, reaching for a silver knife on his desk. 'You will be on the bonfire tonight, peasant, entertainment for the druggie peasants.'

His fingers were closing in on the knife.

Hearing voices when he reached the top of the stairs, Mike pulled his gun out. Turning the handle, he pushed the door open just as the Leader was about to plunge the knife into Mitch's neck.

Quickly, Mike took aim and fired two bullets into the Leader's chest.

For a moment, Mike's and the Leader's eyes met. The Leader's were full of disbelief as he crumbled, hitting the desk as he fell.

Mike hurried over to Shelly. Checking for life, he found a faint pulse and immediately began CPR.

'Is she gonna be all right?' Mitch asked, doubled up in pain, but concern for Shelly on his face.

Ignoring him, Mike carried on administering CPR. After another two minutes, he sat back on his heels and stared down at Shelly's still face.

Mitch sighed, and shook his head.

A moment later, Shelly gasped. Her hand went to her throat, which was covered in bruises.

'Thank God,' Mitch said, as both men nodded their heads.

Her breathing at first was shallow, and Mike helped her to sit up. 'Come on, Shelly. You're going to be just fine.'

'Ambulance? Mitch asked.

'No. Too many questions.'

'I…I'll be all right,' Shelly said, her voice hoarse, as she stared at the Leader's body. 'Is he...?'

'Yes,' Mike replied.

Taking her arms, he helped her onto a chair where, still staring at the Leader, she hugged herself and started rocking back and forth.

'Shock,' Mike mouthed over the top of her head to Mitch, who nodded.

After a minute, Shelly began to settle. 'I don't believe it.'

'Believe it,' Mike replied. 'Now what do we do?'

'We'd planned to let them all go, give the other guards a chance to flee or...' Mitch said.

'Shoot them,' Mike put in.

'Yes.'

'Not a good idea, mate. Half the kids in there would probably have a heart attack, plus the guards have guns. It would be an unnecessary bloodbath. And on a double plus worst case, we end up on a murder charge hiked up by that lot.'

'OK. What do you suggest?'

'We make good our escape. I'm sure those back at the house will have contacts with decent coppers.'

'OK with me.' Mitch looked down at Shelly who nodded her agreement.

'Right, follow me.'

Outside, Mike led them to the vine-covered wall where, in the old monastery, there had been a hidden door. Lifting a portion of vine, he tutted. 'Thought as much. This has got to be the only part that hasn't been reconstructed.'

'What do we do now?' Mitch asked.

'Keep to the plan and get out of here. Shelly,' he cupped his hands, 'if I hoist you up, do you think you can get over?'

'Easy.'

'OK, go for it.'

As Mike hoisted Shelly to the top of the wall, Mitch moved back and took a run at it. Reaching the top at the same time as Shelly, he helped her over and they both dropped to the ground. A few seconds later, Mike joined them.

'Right. We've been lucky up till now, let's hope it keeps up until we reach the car. End of the wall, turn right. Go!'

CHAPTER FORTY-SEVEN

Kristina sat in her room, thinking of Mike and all that lay ahead of them. Aunt May had taken her to one side and told her where Mike had gone, and although she was seriously worried, she knew there was nothing she could do. That was Mike all over, always thinking of others. He would never change.

Would I have him any other way? She smiled.

No, this is the Mike I love.

Whatever comes, we'll face it together.

In the bedroom next door, Brother David sat on the side of his bed resting his head in his hands.

With great difficulty, he had reached a monumental decision. He would leave the order and rejoin the world, having told his God that his services would be more needed outside.

He was sad to leave the order, but he'd thought about it over and over, and Coral had been the catalyst.

Rising, he took a deep breath, squared his shoulders and went downstairs to talk to Aunt May.

He found Danny and Smiler in the sitting room playing cards

and arguing with each other constantly. But, Dave cocked his head, there was a subtle difference. No name-calling, and the odd restrained chuckle from them both.

Hmm, things can only get better.

'Have you seen Aunt May, Smiler?' he asked.

'She's in the garden, Brother David.'

'Please, just Dave.'

Staring at him, Smiler nodded. When he'd passed them on the way to the garden, he said to Danny, 'I knew he was gonna do that, leave the order.'

'How? You a flaming mind reader?'

'Sort of.'

'You better not be cheating.'

'I wouldn't do that.'

Danny stared at him, much the same way Smiler had stared at Dave. 'No, I guess you wouldn't.'

'You believe me?'

'That you can read minds and stuff?' Danny shrugged. 'I guess after everything that's happened, I'll just about believe anything. Er, it's a full moon tonight... Don't say--'

'I'm gonna grow hair and fangs and howl at the moon!'

Danny grinned, shrugged and looked at his cards.

In the garden, Dave watched Aunt May as she pruned some pink roses. They owed so much to this woman, all three of them. She was the only mother he'd ever known. In fact, the whole world owes her, and others before her, a debt that can never be repaid. And now I need to tell her.

'Aunt May.' She looked up. 'We need to talk.'

'Do we bloody have to?' She eyed him suspiciously, guessing what he was going to say.

He gestured with his right hand towards the garden seat, near the pond. 'Please.'

She sighed. 'OK, Dave.'

He did a small double-take. 'You know?'

'Son, it wasn't hard to guess. You were struggling a bit before this business happened, weren't you? It wasn't so hard to see.' She sat down on the seat.

Sitting down next to her, Dave took her hand. 'I won't ask how you know. You've amazed us all in the past, Aunt May.'

Smiling, she patted the top of his hand. 'I won't ask if you're sure, Dave. One thing is certain, you'll have prayed long and hard about this. I guess Coral was the catalyst.'

He sighed. 'Sort of, but it's too soon for anything like that, I'm afraid. Aunt May.'

'Just take it day by day, OK?'

He nodded, then put his arm around her shoulders. 'We all love you, Aunt May.'

Before Aunt May could reply, Ella came running into the garden. 'It's Mitch, Aunt May. They're all safe and out of there.'

Aunt May clapped her hands. 'Thank God!'

Dave grinned as Smiler and Danny came into the garden.

'Does this mean Shelly's on her way back?' Danny asked, his eyes shining with hope.

'It does, Danny.' Aunt May took his hand and squeezed it tight.

Feeling the tears pricking the back of his eyes, Danny nodded, and when Smiler patted his shoulder, he looked at him, managed a weak smile and, still blinking to stop the tears, nodded at him.

'Told you it would be all right,' Smiler said.

'Zip it, Yoda,' Danny cracked, and everyone in the garden laughed.

CHAPTER FORTY-EIGHT

Mitch slipped his phone back in his pocket as they turned the corner, and nearly bumped into Mike, who had stopped dead.

'Shit,' Mike said. 'The car's gone.'

Both Shelly and Mitch looked at him. 'How?' Shelly asked. 'Did you leave the keys in?'

In answer, and still staring at the place where the car should be, Mike took the keys out of his pocket and jangled them.

'Fuck,' Mitch said. 'We're going to have to get off this road.'

'And go where?' Mike asked. 'All we've got is wide open fields.'

But Mitch waved his hands to quiet him. Pulling out his phone. he dialled Ella. 'You're going to have to come and get us, girl. Plan A is in the ditch. And come armed.'

Slipping the phone back in his pocket, he said, 'Follow me, this is the way she'll come.'

Mitch forced a way into the field through the hedgerow.

Following him, with Mike in the rear, Shelly said, 'Is it worth it?' as a twig scratched her arm. 'Ow, bastard,' she muttered, before going on, 'I mean, they're gonna catch us anyhow. I know these guys, they never give up.'

'I think these guys will be long gone shortly, that's why they've nicked the car,' Mike said.

'Wouldn't like to put money on it,' Shelly replied.

They carried on for the next ten minutes in silence, the muddy field from the recent rains hampering their progress, until Mitch, still in the lead, put his right hand up. He looked over the hedge. 'Yes!' He raised his fist in the air. 'It's Ella.' He bent down to find a way through the hedgerow. The next minute, he was lying face down in the mud, with a bullet hole in his brain.

Not seeing this and thinking he'd fell, Shelly laughed, as Mike stepped in front of her. Grabbing Mitch's hand, he felt for a pulse, then looked up at Shelly.

'Get down, now,' he hissed.

'What?' She threw herself onto the ground. 'Oh God, oh dear God, he's dead, isn't he? I thought he'd tripped.'

Sensing her rising hysteria, Mike pulled his gun out and crawled through the mud. He was about to carefully look through the hedgerow when he felt something whiz by him. 'Down, Shelly now. Keep down.'

'But he's dead. He helped me, and he's dead.' She crawled to where Mike was.

'Can you shoot?'

Shelly frowned at him, her gaze flickering to Mitch's lifeless body. After a moment, she nodded, just as more bullets went over their heads.

Without answering, Shelly, knowing what Mike wanted her to do, moved towards Mitch's body. Hastily she rummaged in his pocket until she found his gun.

Watching her, Mike nodded, then turning back he fired a round off in the direction that the bullets had come from, giving a satisfied grin a moment later when he heard a man's voice scream in pain.

Then the sound of more gunfire aimed at their opponents made him grin. 'Ella.'

'Thank God,' Shelly said.

The sound of a car hastily driving off in the other direction, and then the sound of Ella's voice calling them, made them both rise.

'We're here, Ella,' Mike said, brushing aside some of the hedgerow and helping Shelly through.

Ella ran across the road. 'Mitch?'

'I'm afraid he didn't make it, Ella.' Mike grabbed her arms, as she swayed in shock.

Her eyes welled up with tears. She implored Mike, 'Are you sure? Are you really sure?'

Mike nodded again. 'Sorry, Ella.'

'Where is he?'

'Back there.'

As Ella crossed the road, the sound of sirens invaded the sudden silence.

'It's all right,' Ella said. 'They're friendly.'

She ducked under the hedgerow and stared down at Mitch's body. They had known each other for a while now. At first Mitch had been a bit shy, had even turned red every time she'd teased him. But it was only recently it had seemed that they were destined to know each other better.

'Now I'll never know,' she muttered sadly, placing a kiss on Mitch's head.

CHAPTER FORTY-NINE

Tarasov looked in the mirror. What he was about to do fairly went against the grain where the families were concerned. If ever it was found out, he and his would be hunted and hanged.

But not Mike Yorke. He shook his head in wonder. Hours now, and still no sign of him. That stumbling great fool of a legal son would have been caught long before now, and that was a fact. No one looking suspicious on the CCTV cameras, and the agents had nearly finished interviewing the staff. Nothing!

'Impossible,' he said to his reflection. 'Bunch of idiots, the whole fucking lot of them.'

Walking over to the dresser he picked up the address, written on a piece of paper which he'd shoved under a blue glass vase. He was to meet her at a café in Norwich.

He had been corresponding with the woman for over a year now, and working on her side for the last six months. Together, on his information, they had already averted a major war breaking out by diverting a missile, which a certain country had no knowledge of ever having sent, to a desolate spot on the globe.

And now I'm about to meet her!

Should be interesting.

Going down to the hall, he waited while a car was brought round for him, then sent it back and demanded a smaller, less noticeable car without a chauffeur.

The drive into Norwich was uneventful. He passed the same cornfield full of red poppies that Mike and Ella had passed earlier in the day, and took a moment or two to admire the beauty. Something that still amazed him, it was she who had taught him about the ordinary, everyday beautiful things in the world. He'd repressed those feelings for a long, long time, until a dying child had taken the shades from his eyes with her beautiful smile.

He'd known about the opposition, of course he had. The families had known since the beginning. He remembered coming of age and wondering in amazement why, why would the peasants want to be free? Why would they want to live better lives? They had no choice, that was their lot.

Parking the car, he walked down the street to the restaurant, pausing a moment and looking around before he opened the door and slipped in. Once over the threshold he raised one eyebrow. The place was quite luxurious for a peasant joint, he thought, giving it the once-over before he asked the man behind the bar if the woman he had come to meet had arrived.

The barman, a young Polish guy on his first day on the job, pointed to a secluded corner. Tarasov walked over.

The woman sitting at the table had mid-brown hair tied up at the back with a barrette. Her age was hard to tell, although she was no spring chicken. He guessed she was a well-preserved late fifties, maybes more, maybes less, you couldn't always tell, but she was still quite attractive.

He reached the table. 'Hello, I'm--'

'I know who you are. Please sit down, I don't need or want a bloody stiff neck.'

Tarasov was quite stunned for a moment, and fell into his past way of thinking. How dare she address me like that!

A moment later, he was stuttering. 'Me...Mel...Melissa?' His jaw dropped in shock.

CHAPTER FIFTY

Ella, Mike and Shelly arrived back at the safe house. As they walked in Danny, Smiler and Coral looked up. Having decided to play cards with them, Coral put her hand down on the table. She quickly glanced at the open door, then looked at Ella who shook her head. 'He didn't make it, Coral,' Ella said.

'Oh, no.' Coral stood and put her arms around Ella.

Danny, however, was staring at the strange blonde girl. His heart began to beat so loud he could hear it. 'Shelly!'

It took Shelly all of a few seconds to cross the room, then she was in Danny's arms.

'Fancy going for a walk?' Mike said to Smiler.

Smiler jumped up. 'Yeah, Tiny needs to stretch his legs as well. Come on.' Tiny jumped up, and Smiler put the dog's lead on and followed Mike out the door.

'What happened back there?' he asked Mike when they were in the street.

'I guess you could say Mitch was our first casualty of war, Smiler. He was shot through the head.'

'Shit.' Smiler sighed. 'I never met him.'

'Well, for the short time I knew him, he seemed a decent enough bloke.'

'If he worked for Aunt May, he would have been.'

Mike smiled. When they reached the end of the road there was a grassed area, and Smiler let Tiny off for a run.

'You do understand,' Mike said as they watched the dog revelling in his freedom, 'that no one is sure of what is going to happen? It's not just the families we have to fight, it's the agents who have also been living off the fat of the land. Do you think they're gonna go gracefully? Especially when they probably know more about the family businesses than the families do themselves?'

Smiler shook his head. 'It's been a fight for centuries, Mike. But never since the time of Boudicca have we been so organised, instead of fighting back by nibbling here and there at them.'

Mike looked at Smiler. He's got his book head on again, he thought, as Smiler went on.

'Too many wars down the centuries, probably caused by the families themselves, to suit each other and keep those in the arms business going.'

'Couldn't have put it better. So much has become clear since listening to Aunt May.'

'Where is she now? 'Smiler frowned, as if only just missing her.

'She slipped out a while back, said she had someone to meet.'

Bending down, Smiler picked up a stick and threw it for Tiny.

'Do you think she's told us everything?'

'I should hope so…Then again, she's one clever lady. Probably just told us what she thinks we need to know.'

Tiny dropped the stick at Smiler's feet. For a moment, Smiler ignored Tiny and, turning to Mike, said, 'I'm ready, Mike. Whatever it takes, I'm up for it.'

Mike nodded. 'I never doubted it, Smiler… Come on, we best be getting back.'

'OK.' Smiler slipped Tiny's lead on. As they turned to go back, he said, 'What we were saying before, about Aunt May, I reckon she's deffo still got some things up her sleeve.'

PART THREE

CHAPTER FIFTY-ONE

Annya was sitting between Robert and Patrick and listening to Patrick's funny fishing tales. She couldn't help but smile, the first for months, while Robert was near to tears with laughing. When Aunt May came back, and they all said hello, with Shelly looking sheepish and not meeting Aunt May's eyes, Annya rose out of her chair.

'Excuse me, I'm told you're in charge? I want to go home. My grandfather will be really worried. And I have decided that I am going home. To keep me against my will makes you no better than them.'

Aunt May smiled. 'You must be Annya.'

'Yes. Annya Brodzinski.'

'Not to worry, Annya, you'll be going back with us up to Holy Island in the morning.'

Annya gasped. She had not expected it to be so easy. 'But they said...they said I would never be able to go home again, that I would never see my grandfather again!'

'That's the way we had to do it before, child, to save the lives of the victims and their families. But things have bloody changed now all right, and I feel you will be as safe at home as you will be anywhere. A friend is now on her way to inform your grandfather. There is an empty cottage close to mine. It is to be used as a new safe house. I feel you and your grandfather will fit in nicely, and both of you will be a big help.'

'Oh, thank you, thank you so much!' Annya burst into tears, and Coral jumped up to comfort her.

'I have something to say.' Shelly let go of Danny's hand.

Aunt May looked expectantly at her.' Yes, you bloody do.'

Shelly swallowed hard, and glanced at Danny before saying, 'I'm sorry, but I nicked a twenty pound note from your purse... I...I had to do it, I needed money for the bar.'

'It's all right, I knew it was you. Needs must...We can forget about it now you've done the decent thing.'

'But I'll pay you back, promise, as soon as--'

'Forget it, Shelly. It served its purpose all right. Only, the next time, just bloody ask, OK?'

'Oh I will, I will... Sorry again.' Relieved, Shelly sat back down and gripped Danny's hand. He gave her a wink and squeezed back. She had been adamant that she wanted to confess to taking the money, though Danny had said to do it privately. She had not been able to wait, and felt much better now that it was all over.

A knock on the door startled Aunt May, but jumping up, Ella said, 'It's OK, it'll be the pizza man. What, you think I was gonna cook for you lot? No way...'

An hour later, with everyone fed and watered, Aunt May told

them where they would all be living from now on, and what their new roles consisted of. After most had gone to bed, Mike and Kristina sat with Aunt May.

'I met with a man today, Mike. Your father.'

'What?' Mike was shocked. 'How the hell--?'

'I've known Tarasov for a long time, Mike. He has over the last year been very helpful, and has now totally thrown his lot in with ours. Especially... Never mind.'

Mike shook his head. Never mind what? he thought. So much has happened these last few weeks, it's damn hard to get a grip on things, and remember what's what.

Having already told Aunt May about Tarasov and what had happened to him, he said, 'Did you know that he's my father?'

'Yes... There's something else I have to tell you.'

What the fuck now? Mike thought, when they were suddenly interrupted by the sound of the back door opening.

'Hello there.' Tony grinned at them as he walked in.

'You're bloody early,' Aunt May said, lifting her face for a kiss.

Tony kissed her cheek and put his arm around her. 'The traffic was good. So, have you explained everything?' He gave Kristina a smile. 'Nice to see you, Kristina. Back where you belong, eh?'

Kristina returned the smile with a small wave. She had always liked Tony, and remembered picking out a blue tie for him the last Christmas she and Mike were together. She nodded. 'Hopefully for good this time, Tony.'

He turned back to Aunt May and raised an eyebrow, obviously wanting an answer to his question.

'Just about,' she replied.

Mike frowned, not missing the look that had passed between them when Tony asked if she'd explained everything. You're good, Aunt May, he thought, but not good enough to fool me. There's something else going on here, which obviously concerns me.

Standing up, he greeted Tony with a hug, saying, 'Everyone else is in bed.'

'Thought they would be.'

Mike sat back down. 'OK, out with it, both of you. What the hell else is going on?'

Tony hesitated for a moment, then said, 'I take it Aunt May hasn't got round to telling you about the water poisoning business that the families have planned?'

'New one on me,' Mike said, again catching a strange but relieved look that Aunt May threw at Tony.

'What?' asked Kristina, who had pretty much been quiet up until now. 'Water poisoning?'

'It's the latest plan to cut the population down. That and a few others,' Tony said.

'I was going to bloody well tell you all about it when we get home and start the planning. Everything has to be done right, and there are only so many bloody shocks a person can take.'

'OK, we'll leave it till then.' Mike stood up. 'Time for bed.'

'Yes, me too.' Kristina rose, her hand in Mike's.

'See you in the morning, then,' Tony said.

'Night, lovelies.' Aunt May smiled at them both, then patted Mike's arm as he passed.

Nodding, Mike and Kristina headed for the stairs. Although a very large house, the bedrooms were not endless, and with so many people there the sleeping arrangements had to be shared. Mike was in with Dave and Smiler, while Kristina shared a room with Annya and Shelly. They kissed on the landing and said their goodnights. A very disappointed Kristina opened the door of her room, to hear Shelly snoring her head off.

In his room, Mike undressed in the dark then sat on the edge of his single bed. Danny and Smiler slept silently, apart from an odd mutter from Danny, in the double bed facing him.

What the hell is going on now?

There's something. If those two think they can fool me... He shook his head.

Something definitely not right.

He swung his legs onto the bed and pulled the quilt up.

Tomorrow, I'll find out. One way or another.

Downstairs, Tony said, 'Why haven't you told him yet?'

'Has there been any bloody time?'

Tony shrugged. 'He has to know, Aunt May, you know this. You can't keep putting it off. The longer you take, the harder it will be, for both of you.'

She nodded. 'You're right, I know. Just stop bloody harassing me, it's been a hard day.'

Tony took hold of her shoulders. 'Look at me, Aunt May.' She lifted her head. 'Promise me you'll tell him. He deserves the truth.'

'I will, promise...as soon as the time is right.'

'No, Aunt May, that could take forever, and I wouldn't be surprised if he thinks there's something up already. He misses nothing, our Michael Yorke.'

Aunt May smiled. 'It's been so hard, Tony.'

Tony put his arm around her and squeezed. 'Without you, none of this would have happened. It's you who worked so hard to bring everything together, Aunt May. The whole world owes you.'

She nodded. 'And the others before me, let's not forget them.'

'I know.'

'I'm going up to bed now. Goodnight, Tony.' She left him and headed for the stairs.

Tony went into the kitchen and made himself a ham sandwich. Coming back into the sitting room, he switched the television on and loosened his tie before he sat down. He flicked through the numerous channels before deciding on the BBC news.

He smiled at an announcement he'd been expecting, and slowly nodded. A helicopter had crashed over the French border, killing all on board.

'And so it begins,' he muttered.

CHAPTER FIFTY-TWO

Having arrived home three hours earlier, Prince Carl, his Siberian husky dog, Bess, in tow, walked down from his castle to the town. As usual, he stopped outside of Chartres Cathedral to stare in wonder at the magnificent building. His peace was disturbed after a few minutes, however, by the ringing of his mobile phone.

Checking who the call was from, he answered immediately. 'Slone?'

'Yes, the job's done.'

'Good, very good.' Prince Carl quickly hung up. Although the lines were secure, Prince Carl still didn't trust them. A bit like helicopters, he thought, with a smile.

He turned his head in the direction of Count Rene's town house, seeing in his mind's eye a 'For Sale' sign going up outside of it.

'Just might put a bid in for it,' he muttered, pulling on Bess's lead. 'Come on, girl. This way.'

Five minutes later he was sitting outside a coffee house.

As he sipped his coffee, he thought of the American, Slone, and just how good an actor the man was. His performance at the gathering deserved an Oscar at the very least. So many of the families he had fooled into thinking he was against Tarasov.

He patted Bess, as she garnered admiring looks from the people passing by. Bess was his baby. Probably the only baby he would ever have, although even that could be sorted if he wanted it. Or perhaps it would be better to let his line die out.

Plenty of babies in the world to help, he smiled, as he decided he sort of liked this helping business. His smile widened when he saw the young man he had come to meet, walking to his table.

CHAPTER FIFTY-THREE

Mr Brodzinski walked past the water treatment factory. Outside the gates, he stopped to light a cigarette.

His grand-daughter had returned home a few days ago. Since then, they had moved to live on the fantastic Holy Island. He had never been happier, especially as the lady May had told him the whole long story, and asked if he would like to be a part of it.

Would he!

The only downside had been leaving Annya to sort out the house while he jumped on the train to London.

But it was part of the job, and he would do his very best. This was not a war between countries. This was a war against evil and greed, and he was proud to be part of it. His cigarette lit, he strolled slowly on, dragging his left foot behind him, and pulling on the lead of the tiny Jack Russell which the Lady May had got for him as part of his cover, out of the local dogs' home.

Whoever would suspect an old man and his dog of being a spy?

Brodzinski had never, as they put it, been a dog lover, but this little creature had already wrapped its paws around his heart on the journey here. He was seriously thinking of keeping her when he got home. Annya had always wanted a dog. She would be over the moon with this little brown-and-white thing.

He would call her Lily, after his dead wife.

'Come on, Lily,' he said.

He knew he would be on one of those camera things. That was why he'd developed the limp, so that he could be slow. His job was to report in, the minute the tanker left, then to get right back on the next train home.

Already the tanker was seven minutes late. Mr Brodzinski stopped five yards from the gate, and made a big show of rolling his sleeve up to look at his watch. Then he moved on.

Why is it late?

Inside he was fretting.

So many people in place!

Then he heard a heavy engine. He guessed rightly that it was the tanker, he took a quick glance then kept right on walking. Even when it came abreast of him, he didn't look at it. No need to. One thing old age hadn't yet robbed him of was his excellent eyesight, and he had seen that there were three in the cab.

Why would a water tanker need three men?

This is it.

'Got to be,' he muttered.

He waited until the tanker rounded the corner, and he was out of sight of the treatment factory. Before he started to head towards the train station, he pulled his mobile out, and assured the person on the other end the exact time the tanker had left, and that it was heading in the direction they had suspected it would.

Satisfied that he had done the job right, he closed the phone. 'Come on, Lily, we're going home.'

He had failed, however, to note the two cars that had left at five minute intervals, and were now trailing the tanker.

CHAPTER FIFTY-FOUR

Mike snapped his mobile shut and nodded at Tony and Josh. 'It's running seven minutes late, and unescorted.'

Tony frowned. 'Sure it's the right one?'

'Yep, the driver and two passengers.'

'Armed, no doubt,' Josh put in.

'Yeah, well, so are we. This is one toxic tanker that's gonna touch base over my dead body.'

Tony looked at his watch. 'So, an estimated twenty-one minutes until it gets here?'

'Near enough,' Mike answered. 'Best we get into place now.'

'OK.' Tony motioned to Josh with his head for him to follow him over the road where there was tree cover. Once over, Josh moved ten yards down.

Mike jumped down into the ditch at his side of the road. The plan was for Josh, who was an excellent marksman, to shoot the front tyre of the tanker, which would bring it to a stop close to Mike and Tony. When he was in place, Mike sat on a log that was lying in the ditch, and lit a cigarette he had cadged from Josh. Again he marvelled at how things had turned out. Only a few short weeks ago he had been unaware of the real driving force in the world.

'And now here I am, at war with the bastards,' he muttered, watching the smoke from his cigarette spiral into the sky.

And Smiler... What a change there!

Who would have believed it?

The cigarette, now in danger of burning his fingers, was flung to the ground and stamped on. He looked at his watch. Still nearly fifteen minutes to go.

And to top it all, me and Kristina back together. He shook his head in pleased amazement at the way things had turned out.

I knew as soon as I saw her that I wanted her back. Why the hell didn't I just tell her then, bloody idiot that I am?

He looked at his watch again. Shit! Three minutes!

OK, this is it.

He strained his ears. Another two minutes went by before he heard the sound of a heavy vehicle pulling up the bank. Mike looked over the top of the ditch. There were clumps of grass where he knew he could see and not be seen. Just before the tanker came into view, he heard the sound of Josh's pistol. A few seconds later he saw the tanker. It was lurching from side to side as the driver tried to bring it to a halt. Mike could see the white faces of the three men as they stared in front of them.

Just in front of Mike, it finally came to a stop. In moments, Mike was up and running to the side of the cab, yanking the door open at exactly the same time as Tony pulled the driver's door open. The man on Mike's side immediately put his hands up and started babbling in Spanish.

'OK, I get the message, just get out of the fucking cab,' Mike snarled, gesturing for him to move with his gun. 'And leave the weapon.' The man obliged and Mike, quickly glancing at them, said to the man in the middle, who also had his hands up, 'You an' all. Move it, now.'

He had both men lying on the ground when he heard two rapid shots. Quickly, he moved back one step to the cab. The driver was slumped over the wheel, blood dripping onto the floor, and Tony was holding his arm and gritting his teeth as blood soaked through his jacket.

'What the...?'

'The bastard shot me. So much for Aunt May's "Try to do it peaceful" plan.'

'You gonna be all right?'

Tony nodded. 'It's the top of my arm, think it's just nicked me.'

'Phew.' Mike heaved a sigh of relief.

It was short-lived, though. A few seconds later, they both looked downhill when they heard the sound of not one, but two cars heading their way. Quickly, Mike snapped a pair of handcuffs on each of the men.

'Where the fuck's Josh?' Mike said, looking across at Tony.

Before he could answer, they heard rapid gunfire, then the sound of it being returned. The cars stopped, and three men jumped out of each car. Four ran into the trees where Josh was, and two ran up the hill. Mike took aim and fired.

The first man fell, just as the second one fired at Mike, who dived into the cab. One of the handcuffed men on the ground screamed as Mike climbed across the cab towards Tony, and pushed the dead driver out. Tony started firing at the now retreating man. Five shots later, just as he was about to go into the trees, the man went down.

For a brief moment there was silence. Then they heard gunshots from the trees.

'You stay here,' Mike said, as he reloaded his gun.

Both he and Tony looked round when they heard another car coming at them from the other way. Tony raised his gun.

'No,' Mike said, pushing Tony's gun down. 'It's Patrick and Dave with the new tyre and the gear to change it for the tanker.'

'Thank God,' Tony breathed, as both men jumped out of the car.

'Follow me.' Mike waved them on as they both drew their guns. Quickly they followed him into the woods.

Once among the trees, they followed the sound of shouting between the gunshots. Patrick was the first to fire his gun, his keen eyes spotting a man running through the undergrowth. He went down immediately.

Suddenly, all the guns were pointing in their direction. After a five-minute standoff, one man shouted, 'Enough.'

'Keep down,' Mike said, as he moved forward. 'OK, gun on the ground and hands where I can see them...Move.'

An hour later, the tanker and its contents were in a safe environment, where people knew exactly how to neutralize the danger.

Mike and Tony had stayed behind to watch the process, satisfied that it was over they headed towards Tony's car.

'Well,' Mike said with a grin. 'I guess this is the start of the end.'

Looking at him over the top of the car, Tony nodded. 'At last, the dream that people started all those centuries ago, we hopefully will bring to fruition.'

'Not hopefully Tony, but truly.' Mike smiled. 'The final countdown has at last - finally began!'

Together they headed home.

EPILOGUE

Two days later, Tony, his arm in a sling, sat facing Aunt May across the breakfast table. Rarely seen in a t-shirt, he had borrowed one of Mike's pale blue ones, as he was adamant no one could tie his ties like he could. Mike had grumbled good-naturedly, saying both he and Dave needed to do some shopping, as between them he would soon have nothing left to wear.

Tony had been staring at Aunt May, knowing full well that she was avoiding any small talk. He shook his head. Time to get it over with.

'It's time, Aunt May. You can't put it off any longer, I'm sure he suspects something.'

'I bloody know.' She lifted her head from her newspaper and looked at him. 'Today, OK.'

'Promise.'

Mike walked in, passed their table and went over to the toaster. 'Morning,' he said, as he picked up two slices of wholemeal bread and dropped them in the toaster.

He came and sat at the table and before he asked just what the hell was going on, Aunt May spoke.

Smiling, she said, 'I hope you've got nothing planned for today, Mike.'

'Why?' he asked, before taking a bite out of his toast.

'I need a lift to Finchale Priory.'

'Where?'

'It's just off Chester-le-Street. You know, near Houghton-le-Spring.'

'I know where it is. I should have said, why there?'

'Something I have to do. Plus I thought we could spend the day together.'

Mike looked at Tony, who lifted his bandaged arm as an excuse not to take her.

Mike sighed. He had never been able to refuse her anything. 'OK, soon as I've finished this.'

'Good. I'll go and get ready.' Aunt May hurried out of the room.

'Fancy coming along for the ride?' Mike asked Tony.

'No, not today, feeling a bit under the weather. Have a good day.' Tony rose and left the room.

'Hmm,' Mike muttered. as he watched Tony, through the open door, taking the stairs two at a time. 'Doesn't look much like you're under the weather to me!'

He finished his toast just as Aunt May, dressed in a pink suit with a flowery blouse, came back in. She checked for something in her extremely large cream shoulder bag, before putting the strap over her shoulder and looking expectantly at Mike.

'OK.' He fished his keys out of his pocket. 'Let's be off.'

Two hours later, they arrived at Finchale Priory. Mike helped Aunt May out of the car and, after locking it, they walked over to the priory.

'Cup of tea?' Aunt May asked.

'Yeah, why not.' Mike was staring at the magnificent ruins of the priory. He'd forgotten how just big the place was. He remembered Aunt May bringing the three of them here with a picnic at least two or three times a year, when they were kids.

'Find a bench,' Aunt May said. 'I'll bring them over.'

Mike nodded. Still transfixed by the beauty of the place, he walked over to a bench near the river and sat down. A few minutes later, Aunt May joined him and put a tray with two cups of tea, an assortment of chocolate biscuits and a pack of ham sandwiches on the bench.

'Thought you might be a bit bloody peckish. Long drive and all that. I know you like ham, really should have made a picnic.'

Smiling, Mike tore the cellophane off the pack. He offered one of the sandwiches to Aunt May.

'No, thanks. I would rather have a bloody biscuit.' She dipped her chocolate biscuit into her tea.

'So, what the hell's going on, Aunt May?' Mike said suddenly, startling her for a moment.

She looked over at the priory and, ignoring his question, said, 'Many, many years ago, in the twelfth century, St Godric came to live here. Finchale remained a priory until the fifteenth century. But it has always kept its secret. The one St Godric brought with him from Norfolk.'

'OK, you got me. What secret?'

'Finish eating and I'll show you.'

'Aunt May, you minx,' Mike laughed, as he ate the remains of his sandwich. 'OK.' He said, a few minutes later.

She looked at him as she got up from the bench. 'This way.' She linked her arm through his as they headed up the grassy slope. When they reached the priory, they walked through room after room until they came to the far side.

'It's here where St Godric hid the book. It's never been disturbed since. The key has been passed down the generations to the keeper of the book.' She paused a moment. Taking a deep breath, she went on, 'When the keeper reaches a certain age, they are obliged to pass the key on to the next keeper.' She paused for a moment and looked up at him. 'That's you, Mike Yorke. As my son, you are the next keeper of the book.'

Mike felt his knees wobble. Had she just said what he thought she'd said?

Aunt May turned. 'You heard right, Mike. You are my real son. I am your birth mother.'

'But, how… What about Tarasov?'

'He is your father.'

'But--'

'Simply put, Mike, I was once one of Tarasov's slaves. He knew me as Melissa... I escaped. I had to give you up so that Tarasov bloody well wouldn't find you. Those days he would have handed you right over to the families, you would have ended up pretty much the way Smiler did. But I managed to get a job in Social Services, close to the home you grew up in, until I judged it safe to get you out of there.' She shrugged. 'By then, I'd also grown to love Tony and Dave, who were both desperately in need of a home.'

'Stop.' Mike put his hand up. 'Too much.' He shook his head. 'I can't believe that you've been lying to me all these years.' He stared at her, his eyes full of pain.

'I'm sorry, Mike.' She put her hand on his arm, but Mike hastily shrugged it off.

'I need time.' He turned quickly and walked away from her, heading towards the river.

Sadly, biting back the tears Aunt May watched him go.

Then unable to help herself she began to sob.

She had known that it would not be easy, that Mike could possibly reject her, and also the role of keeper of the book. But she'd had to wait until Tarasov was completely on board.

An hour later, she was still sitting on the bench when she spotted Mike coming towards her over the footbridge. She had prayed and prayed over the last hour for Mike to see the bigger picture, and realise that she had done the only thing she could. A few minutes later, he was sitting opposite her.

'Well?' Aunt May stared into Mike's dark eyes. She'd lived this moment over and over in her dreams, and now that the time had come she was terrified.

'These…these people have touched and destroyed so many lives.'

Aunt May swallowed hard as Mike hesitated a moment.

'I guess, in the circumstances, you did the only thing you could…Mother.'

Bursting into tears, Aunt May stood and reached out for her son, remembering all the years she had waited to hear him call her 'Mother'.